GW01003396

NESTHÄKCHEN AND THE WORLD WAR

Nesthäkchen and the World War

First English Translation of the German Children's Classic

Else Ury
Translated, introduced, and annotated by Steven Lehrer

iUniverse, Inc.
New York Lincoln Shanghai

Nesthäkchen and the World War
First English Translation of the German Children's Classic

Copyright © 2006 by Steven Lehrer

All rights reserved. No part of this book may be used or reproduced by any means, graphic, electronic, or mechanical, including photocopying, recording, taping or by any information storage retrieval system without the written permission of the publisher except in the case of brief quotations embodied in critical articles and reviews.

iUniverse books may be ordered through booksellers or by contacting:

iUniverse
2021 Pine Lake Road, Suite 100
Lincoln, NE 68512
www.iuniverse.com
1-800-Authors (1-800-288-4677)

ISBN-13: 978-0-595-39729-7 (pbk)
ISBN-13: 978-0-595-84136-3 (ebk)
ISBN-10: 0-595-39729-8 (pbk)
ISBN-10: 0-595-84136-8 (ebk)

Printed in the United States of America

CONTENTS

▼

List of Illustrations

Introduction

A recent survey of German women revealed that 55% had read Else Ury's Nesthäkchen books. Even more had heard them read over the radio or had seen the television serialization. These stories show an ordinary girl growing up, and attempt to explain to children why a girl is so different from a boy, and so interesting too. At the end of the tenth volume of the series, the delighted reader comes away with the answer: Girls aren't so different. Nesthäkchen's adventures had another attraction for children. They were more factual and showed more of daily life than did other children's stories of the time. There was plenty of conflict, yet it was good natured and funny. Even the worst situations had agreeable resolutions.

But like the popular Wild West books of German author Karl May, the Nesthäkchen books have not traveled well. Else Ury tried but failed to have her own English translation published in the late 1930's. A Dutch translation a few years earlier was hardly more successful. Yet in Germany, the Nesthäkchen series is a perennial best seller. As of 1992, seven million copies were in print. German bookstores invariably reserve a special rack in the children's department for Ury's Nesthäkchen books.

Else Ury was born in Berlin, November 1, 1877, the third child of third generation Berlin merchant Jews. Her large, well-to-do, close-knit bourgeois family provided a loving environment. The experiences of her own happy childhood, as well as her observation of the growth of her sisters, brothers, nephews, and nieces, inspired Else Ury to later write her family and youth books.

Her grandfather, Levin Elias Ury, was director of the synagogue in the Heidereutergasse in central Berlin. Her parents, who lived in Charlottenberg, were no more religious than most of the Christians in the neighborhood. But the Urys never hid their Jewish origins.

One older brother, Ludwig, studied law, while another, Hans, studied medicine, and Else's younger sister Käthe became a teacher. Although women's needs for education and a profession to secure independence were later a recurring theme in her books, Else Ury herself pursued no professional studies.

In 1900 Else Ury began publishing travel reports and stories in the Vossiche Zeitung, a Berlin newspaper, under a pen name. Because a father was supposed to support his unmarried daughters, if a girl still living at home earned money by writing, social convention forced her to disguise her identity.

Else's father, Emil Ury, was a tobacco products manufacturer, who produced snuff and chewing tobacco. When cigarette popularity soared around the turn of the century, snuff and chewing tobacco sales declined precipitously. Faced with economic ruin, Emil Ury tried to prevail upon Else to marry the son of a rich cigarette manufacturer, with the hope that a merger of the two family companies would follow. But Else resisted this scheme, and remained single her entire life.

In 1906 Else Ury had her first modest literary success with *Educated Girl*, a novel dealing with the very controversial subject of higher education for women. Indeed, regular women's university studies were first permitted in Prussia only in 1908. Although Emil Ury's business had gone bankrupt, Else was able to help support her family with book royalties.

Her breakthrough to bestseller status came with her Nesthäkchen books. Germans call a spoiled child or family pet a *Nesthäkchen*. Else Ury's Nesthäkchen is a Berlin doctor's daughter, Annemarie Braun, a slim, golden blond, quintessential German girl. The ten book series follows Annemarie from infancy (*Nesthäkchen and Her Dolls*) to old age and grandchildren (*Nesthäkchen with White Hair*). Despite Else Ury's Jewish background, she makes no references to Judaism in the Nesthäkchen books.

Nesthäkchen and the World War (1916), the fourth and most popular volume in the series, sold 300,000 copies. Else Ury wrote the fifth and sixth volumes, *Nesthäkchen's Teenage Years,* in 1919, and *Nesthäkchen Flies From the Nest* in 1923. She intended to stop there, with Nesthäkchen's marriage, but her readers simply wouldn't let her. Distraught girls inundated her Berlin publisher, Meidingers Jugendschriften Verlag, with a flood of letters pleading for more Nesthäkchen stories. Else Ury obliged her young fans with four more Nesthäkchen books.

On November 1, 1927, Else Ury's fiftieth birthday, Meidingers Jugendschriften Verlag gave their celebrated author a large reception, and announced the publication of an expensively bound new edition of all ten Nesthäkchen books. The series had been an immense success, and even the head of the company, Kurt Meidinger, was on hand to praise Else Ury and her work. The Adlon Hotel, the most elegant in Berlin, catered the affair, which was attended by many reporters, and chronicled in German newspapers the next day. In the meantime, Meidingers had established a special post office box for Nesthäkchen correspondence. Readers sent both letters and pictures they had drawn for the stories. Else Ury answered all mail monthly and, from time to time, held parties for her Nesthäkchenkinder, with cake and chocolate, in the garden of her house. Many of the parties were the subject of newspaper stories.

Despite her literary success, Else Ury lived quietly, and didn't consider the details of her own life to be especially noteworthy. In 1926, with money from her books, she bought a vacation house in the Riesengebirge area of Krummhübel, which she named "House Nesthäkchen." Here she and her family spent many summer and winter vacations.

In Else Ury's last book, *Youth to the Fore*, published in 1933, the author tried to put a good face on Hitler's rise to power. The book dealt with overcoming the economic crisis and unemployment, restoring order with a firm hand, and strengthening Germany. No one is certain whether Ury was politically naive and had been seduced by Nazi propaganda, or whether her publisher, to please the regime, had obediently altered the text.

As a Jew, Else Ury was excluded from the Reich Chamber of Writers in 1935, which meant she was no longer allowed to publish. By 1936, most of her relatives had emigrated, and her brother Hans had committed suicide. She herself did not want to leave Germany. "If my co-religionists are staying, then I too must have courage, character, and strong decisiveness, and be willing to share their fate," she said. Also, she had to care for her 90-year-old mother, Franziska, who in photographs bears a remarkable resemblance to Sigmund Freud's mother, Amalie.

Else Ury traveled to London, in 1938, for a short visit to her nephew, Klaus Heymann, but ignored his pleas for her to stay in England. She returned to Berlin and remained until the Nazis deported her. Her mother died in 1940.

Until 1933, Else Ury lived in Kantstraße 30, then at Kaiserdamm 24. In 1939 she was forced to move to a "Jew house," a former Jewish old age home in Solingerstraße 10, where the Gestapo collected Jews for deportation. On January 6, 1943, she had to fill out a declaration of all her possessions, and with one valise and a few articles of clothing, report for resettlement. She was ordered to present herself at a collection point, Großer Hamburgerstraße 26, to wait for transport. On January 11, 1943, she signed a release, turning over all her property to the German Reich. German officials proceeded to sell off everything she owned.

On January 12, 1943, the 65-year-old Else Ury was taken to the railroad station at Berlin Grunewald, along with 1,190 other Berlin Jews, packed into a boxcar, and deported to Auschwitz-Birkenau. A day later, SS doctors selected 127 men from her transport for labor. SS guards murdered Else Ury and the other Jews in the gas chamber.

After 1945, Else Ury's books were heavily edited and many contemporaneous or historical references removed. In 1983, there was a six-part television serialization of the Nesthäkchen books. Finally, half a century after her death, her millions of women readers learned the details of her dreadful fate.

A group of high school students from the Robert Blum Gymnasium in Berlin-Schöneberg discovered the exact date of Else Ury's death on a visit to Auschwitz in 1995. They also found there her battered valise, labeled with her name and Berlin address. The valise and other objects and documents relating to her life were exhibited in Berlin until 2002, when they were returned to the museum at Auschwitz. They are heartbreaking to see.

Of all the millions of murders the Nazis committed, Else Ury's stands out. Could anyone imagine the British murdering AA Milne a few years after he had written Winnie the Pooh?

NESTHÄKCHEN AND THE WORLD WAR

Nesthäkchen and the World War is a difficult book for Germans. After World War II it was not republished with the other nine Nesthäkchen volumes. The Meidingers catalogue stated that the book was not a war story or a "hurrah tale." But it is by no stretch of the imagination an anti-war book, either.

With the country nothing but a heap of rubble in 1945, the Germans wanted no more to do with the sentiments that had brought them to such a pass. High on the list were love for the fatherland, exaggerated respect for the military, and enthusiasm for war.

These sentiments were easy to excise from most of the Nesthäkchen books. For example, in *Nesthäkchen in the Children's Sanatorium*, the volume preceding *Nesthäkchen and the World War*, Else Ury describes a German submarine, which Annemarie watches as it disappears underwater. "Then it was certainly a submarine, Annemarie," says a companion, "that can dive and remain submerged for hours without anyone seeing it. We discovered the submarine to be a weapon for war at sea. God grant that we will never need to use it." In the revised version of

Nesthäkchen in the Children's Sanatorium issued in 1950, the submarine is not mentioned.

But no amount of rewriting could ever remove all objectionable material from *Nesthäkchen and the World War*, as it is too integral to the plot. Despite its enormous prewar success, no German language publisher would touch this volume.

Else Ury never caught on in the English speaking world, most likely because when she was at the height of her popularity, either the Germans were our blood enemy, or the carnage of World War I was too recent for anyone to want to read about the mind-set of the people who initiated it. Today, though, Else Ury's books, particularly *Nesthäkchen and the World War*, present a charming evocation of a long-vanished time and place. Germany, a solid democracy, has been our friend and staunch ally for more than half a century. A modern reader feels deep sympathy for the trusting, good-hearted, generous people whom a fatuous Kaiser and a pack of bungling, inept diplomats had thrust into a horrific war. Moreover, Else Ury's love for Germany now seems quite poignant and sad, in light of what happened to her.

The depiction of Nesthäkchen's abuse of Vera, a Polish-speaking refugee child whom the author introduces in Chapter 10 of *Nesthäkchen and the World War*, is quite upsetting to some German readers. Nesthäkchen mercilessly excludes the kindly, pathetic Vera from her group and turns her into a school pariah.

In fact, Else Ury has rendered Nesthäkchen as a more believable character because of her treatment of Vera. Nesthäkchen's mean streak makes her quite human. And of course, schoolchildren similarly brutalize each other today, especially their peers who cannot conform to group pressure, witness the Columbine High School massacre. Enid Blyton, the English children's writer with whom Else Ury is frequently compared, and who is very popular with German girls, depicts situations analogous to Vera's.

More important, the device is indispensable for the development of the plot and leads to the shocking, ringing climax in Chapter 16, one of the most moving sections of the entire book. Else Ury also skillfully employs exposition and plot to develop scenes that are laugh-out-loud funny, followed by others that are highly melodramatic. *Nesthäkchen and the World War* holds the reader's attention from beginning to end. It is not surprising that it was the most popular volume in the series.

And the book conveys a timeless lesson, for children as well as adults, about the nature of war. Wars often begin with an outpouring of patriotic sentiment. World War I started this way, and Else Ury's description of German war-euphoria in 1914 is chilling. But Nesthäkchen quickly comes to recognize the hardships and horrors of war, the dislocations, the pathetic refugees, the scarcity of food, the combat deaths of favorite teachers, relatives, and friends. In *All Quiet on the Western Front*, Erich Maria Remarque describes World War I more horrifically, but he was writing from the battlefield. Ury's depiction of the war as seen from Berlin, though gentler, is as powerful as Remarque's. When *Nesthäkchen and the World War* ends, in mid 1916, battle had become mass slaughter. Else Ury, unlike Remarque, could not bear the pain of writing about it further.

CHAPTER 1

▼

NESTHÄKCHEN LEARNS TO MAKE SACRIFICES

It was red hot on the balcony. Even the shady side was not spared the intense heat of the August sun, which was cooking the Berlin streets.

An old lady's head with silver hair and a golden-blonde child's head were bent over gray knitting. Industriously the needles clicked in the hands of the elderly lady, as the child's fingers advanced the knitting haltingly. But the sun-tanned little hands moved more and more lazily, until finally Annemarie flung the scarcely begun wristband to the stone floor.

"Pooh–I'm choking!" The sea-tanned, round child's face, which raised itself gaspingly, was no less red than the fire-red muslin fabric, which the eleven-year old girl wore. "Dear Grandmother, what will our soldiers do with a thick wrist band in this stifling heat? I think I can quietly put off my knitting until winter." Without further ado, the little dog Puck began to bite and tear the wool fabric. Pieces of fabric blew into the air and off among the chimneys of Berlin.

"Dear child, if we don't take charge of our fingers before autumn, our poor soldiers will freeze in the Russian cold. We must be industrious in summer so that we've finished everything by winter." Grandmother's fingers moved more rapidly, as though she had to clothe an entire regiment against the Russian cold.

"But I'm so hot! I have to get used to the Berlin air again. When you've been in the Baltic for a year, where there's always a fresh sea wind blowing, the city air presses on your head, as Father always said."

"Now listen to me, my dear," said Grandma, turning her kindly face to the pretty blond head. "Don't you think that our noble boys in field gray, who joyfully go to war, are suffering, too, in the August heat? Haven't you seen their heavy knapsacks? Don't you think that their helmets press more heavily on their heads than the big city air? And yet the brave boys celebrate and sing, in spite of the fact that the daylong trip to the front in hot narrow train cars is no pleasure. You saw this yourself, my child, as we accompanied your father to the station. Do we want our bold warriors to be ashamed of those who stay at home? Don't we want to endure some discomforts for them? They are willing to give their lives for us, to sacrifice everything for us." Grandmother's dear, clear eyes looked intently into the blue eyes of the little girl, who cast hers down, ashamed.

"If I were grown, I would certainly also sacrifice myself for our fatherland," said Annemarie finally, with unaccustomed reflection. "I would become a nurse and care for the wounded like Aunt Lenchen. Oh, Grandmother, that would be beautiful! Just think, I wouldn't have to leave Daddy, who I haven't seen for a whole year. I would go to war with him—oh, that would be wonderful." The radiant eyes of the little girl beamed longingly.

"My dear child, in these challenging times, you don't have to be a grownup and do great things in order to support Germany. Children also can make sacrifices that can help. Nothing is too small—the tiniest pebble that you carry to the great war-work edifice is valuable." As she spoke, Grandmother turned her eyes to the wristband that Annemarie had thrown to the floor, and with which Puck was now occupied.

Annemarie bent down quickly and snatched the shredded woolen band away from her four-legged friend.

"If I were a boy, I could do something other than sit here with some dumb knitting. Look how well Hans is doing as a guide. He can stay at the railroad station the whole day and take care of the soldiers passing through. That's much better than torturing yourself with lumpy wristbands." In vain the child tried to bring some order to the mess Puck had made of the shredded fabric.

Grandmother had to console her.

"I don't think Hans is having such an easy time in his railroad station work during these hot August days. He comes home at night tired and overheated. But, my child, whatever we have to do is important, even if it is difficult for us. We have to set aside our own desires; we can only think about the welfare of our fatherland and our brave defenders. Otherwise, we are not making a proper sacrifice."

Grandma sighed inaudibly. Indeed, she herself had learned to suppress her own longings during these difficult August days. Both of her sons-in-law had been conscripted. One, a Silesian farmer, had become a reserve officer in the east. Annemarie's father, Doctor Braun, was now an army doctor with the troops in France. The worries plaguing Grandmother about her conscripted family were shared with thousands of German mothers. But another, larger concern tore at her heart.

What was the fate of her daughter Elsbeth, Annemarie's mother?

The elderly lady had had no peace since both France and England, in a disgraceful manner, had declared themselves to be Germany's enemies. At the outbreak of war, Annemarie's mother was visiting relatives in England. Would it be possible for her to return home unimpeded? Or would she be held in England as an enemy alien? Luckily the child, Doctor's Nesthäkchen, sensed none of Grandmother's fear and agitation. The fear surfaced every time the doorbell rang, and Grandmother hoped against hope that Annemarie's mother had come back. Or at least that there was some word of her.

But even this worry the elderly lady subordinated to her fears for the threatened fatherland. Surrounded by jealous enemies, how would Germany, despite her bravery and inspiration, manage to prevail? As fabric glided from one needle to the other, one ominous thought after another glided through Grandmother's mind.

Even in the young head of the grandchild, unpleasant thoughts arose, though not as troubling as those of her grandmother.

In the confusion of events, Doctor's Nesthäkchen was able to orient herself only with difficulty. Everything had happened so quickly. The flight from the Baltic spa Wittdün, where she had spent a year in a children's sanatorium recovering from a serious illness. The jarring change from the quiet sanatorium to the noisy war tumult in Berlin. Saying goodbye to her beloved father over a few hours, after she had been separated from him for a year. From a packed troop train, in field gray uniform, he had said *auf Wiedersehen* to his Nesthäkchen. On the side of the car was a jokey sign, "Express train to Paris."

At home everything had changed. Neither Father nor Mother was there, and the children felt their absence sorely. Annemarie often ran to her mother's window seat, the way she always had when she had something important to tell her. But the window seat was empty. At other times Annemarie thought, when she heard the front door, that Father had returned from his clinic, and she longed to run and greet him, as she always had.

Was she not sacrificing enough for the fatherland by being without her parents for so long?

To be sure, Grandmother had come immediately to care for the three orphaned children. But because of the declaration of war, the agitated lady overwhelmed them, especially the two youngest, Klaus and Annemarie, whom she always wanted by her side. The wild Klaus managed to escape her. Nesthäkchen, in contrast, tried to make things easy for dear Grandmother, who was accustomed to the quiet life. But this accommodation was not always agreeable to Annemarie, who, during her year in the Baltic, had become accustomed to wandering freely in the garden, the beach, and the meadow.

Moreover, Annemarie, who had looked forward to being with her older brother, was again quite disappointed. Hans, her favorite sibling, was always busy as a guide at the railroad station, serving the fatherland. He had much more important things to do than occupy himself with his young sister. Even Klaus was gone most of the time, following the troops around in the field, where they awaited new war dispatches, and where people were always coming and going. Grandma wished she could keep Klaus on a leash, as she did Puck.

Only Hanne, the cook, remained as society for Nesthäkchen, who, in the children's sanatorium had always been surrounded by children of her own age. But the war had completely invested the head of the old cook. She talked of nothing but the Russians and famine.

If only Margot Thielen, Annemarie's best school friend, were home. Margot lived in the same building as Doctor's Nesthäkchen. From the tenth class onward, Annemarie and Margot had been close. But the curtains over Margot's windows were tightly closed. No matter how much Annemarie stared at them, they would not rise. The military trains had probably prevented the Thielen family from returning home after their vacation. But no doubt Margot, an industrious student, would be back when school started. For this reason, Annemarie looked forward to going back to school, even though she enjoyed vacation at least as much. Also she wanted to be with her other school friends, whom she had not seen for a year. Representing Annemarie's father, Grandmother had written to the school director, and enrolled Annemarie in the sixth class.

The knitting needle stuck to Annemarie's hands, so tightly was it pressed between her fingers. She had knitted for ten full minutes, and no wrist warmer. Annemarie cast a puzzled glance at the tower clock, which was visible from her balcony. Still a half-hour before coffee. A true vexation: could the soldiers really demand such a sacrifice from her? Would nothing release her from this tedious knitting?

In her basket chair, Grandmother had nodded off, abetted by the heat. She had sacrificed her midday nap to work for the soldiers and to keep an eye on Nesthäkchen. Of course, old ladies knit with pleasure, but when you are eleven years old…

Should Annemarie act like Klaus, and sneak off?

No, no, she couldn't do that, and throw Grandmother into a fit of anxiety. The old lady would think that Annemarie had fallen from the balcony. What an awful way to pay Grandma back for all her efforts.

But—listen—military music, accompanied by the clattering sound of marching feet on the pavement. Annemarie flung her knitting in the corner and ran to the balcony railing.

The tumult awakened Grandma abruptly from her nap, and she leaped to the balcony rail. Fearfully she seized Annemarie, who was leaning perilously far over the street.

With *Gloria-Victoria,* the blare of bugles and the clatter of drums, regiment after regiment, all bedecked with flowers, marched to the nearby railroad station. At the sides of the men were wives and children, who were leading their sons, husbands, and fathers. From dawn to dusk the songs of the marching troops broke through the otherwise quiet street, providing a lovely change for Nesthäkchen.

Suddenly all balconies were full. From every open window, heads, hands, and cloths waved good luck to the soldiers.

Nesthäkchen, too, greeted the men with her red-rimmed cloth, which still held a knitting needle. Grandmother finally had to pull her away. How easily the girl could tumble from the balcony. But the precariousness of her position worried Annemarie not a whit. All her boredom had vanished. From the geraniums and petunias growing on the balcony, she plucked the flowers that had bloomed in the August sun and tossed them to the marchers in field gray. Grandmother was horrified.

"Child! Child! You destroyed the beautiful pots of flowers," she admonished.

"For our warriors we stay-at-homes must make sacrifices," said the child eagerly, using the same words the elderly lady had spoken from her heart a few moments before.

Grandmother had to smile at the humorous girl. But the smile died on her lips. "My cloth, my handkerchief—" Only by a hair, Annemarie missed tumbling to the street after the fluttering handkerchief.

"I'm back." Before Grandmother could take hold of Annemarie, the handkerchief had sailed to the ground.

One of the soldiers in field gray, smiling, had speared the handkerchief with his rifle, from which it fluttered like a flag.

Annemarie, who never wore a hat or coat on the street in Wittdünn, dashed out similarly attired after the fluttering handkerchief. Over the music, she could not make the soldier understand that she wanted the handkerchief back. Or did the soldier pretend not to understand, as a joke? Finally she gave up and marched next to the "flag carrier," as she began to sing the soldiers' song:

> The little birds in the forest,
> They sing so wonder—wonderfully,
> In the homeland, in the homeland,
> We will see them again.

With a thumping heart, Grandmother watched the little red dot in all the field-gray move further and further away. Would the child come home again?

Finally, at the end of the long street, before the gray human line bent around the corner, Nesthäkchen got her property back. With long strides she raced to her parents' home.

So—that was certainly a cheerful lift at just the right time. Annemarie felt well refreshed after her brief journey.

Grandmother felt differently.

"Child, child, how I worried about you—without a hat, with only your apron, you ran into the street. A well brought up girl does not do that." The kindly grandmother took care not to appear angry, so that her words would have even more impact.

"Oh, granny, if you're always worrying about us, you won't have a happy life here. Perhaps you could become less anxious, because your anxiety is all in vain."

But then Annemarie reached for her knitting. The soldiers, who went so joyfully to war, should not freeze. Perhaps the nice soldier, who gave her back the handkerchief, would get the wrist warmer. Nesthäkchen tortured herself to work on the thick woolen material, little beads of sweat appearing on her brown forehead. She didn't stop until Hanne appeared with the coffee pot. Grandmother stroked Annemarie's blond hair: "So, we have done enough for today, dear one."

"Hurrah—I have sacrificed enough for today," Nesthäkchen exclaimed so lustily that a bold sparrow on the balcony rail fluttered fearfully away.

CHAPTER 2

▼

EXTRA! EDITION

Hanne was a devoted older lady, who had carried Doctor's Nesthäkchen in her arms. But now Hanne was beside herself with agitation, after talking with her friends the greengrocer, the milkman, and the porter. She no longer knew what she was doing.

Even today, much to Nesthäkchen's covert amusement, Hanne had put the silver soup ladle next to Grandmother's pot of coffee.

"Ay, Hanne, should I pour the coffee with the ladle?" Both grandmother and granddaughter laughed at the comment.

"No, we should use the ladle as a coffee spoon to stir the sugar in the cup," said Annemarie happily.

"These Russians, they are making me completely crazy," said Hanne, shaking the pot as she reached for the oversize coffee spoon.

"Just wait, Hanne. When the Russians are right outside Berlin, then it will be something else," said Nesthäkchen teasingly, knowing Hanne's fear of Russians.

There was a fiery outburst.

"*Good heavens*, you sinful child. The porter joins his regiment today. He told me the Cossacks are supposed to be outside Küstrin already.[1] This morning the

---

1. Küstrin (now Kostrzyn, western Poland) is a small town 85 km east of Berlin.

milkman clearly heard canon fire. And the green grocer believes the Russians are coming for sure, since we have too many enemies. We can dispose of one enemy, but not three." Hanne stretched her thick red arms, as though she had inherited the task of defending Germany against all its enemies.

"Calm yourself, Hanne." Grandmother, who had felt the same anxiety a few moments earlier, now looked thoroughly amused. "Our brave men in field gray already know how to protect us from a Russian visit. We must rely on them in these difficult times, and above all Our Helper Above."

"God, of course, but if we only had the Doctor and our gracious lady at home, then I wouldn't be in such a dismal mood. I'm so torn up at the moment, I feel responsibility for the whole family. Because Grandma is not a youngster any more. And I've been in this house more than ten years."

"Yes, yes, Hanne, we know that you mean well." Grandmother, who had enough worries already, desired that her agreeable coffee hour not be disturbed.

But the outbreak of war had loosened Hanne's tongue. Once she began to talk, she didn't stop.

"I want to add something else. Everybody says famine is coming. They're madly buying up everything. You want something from the merchant on the corner, you're out of luck, because they've already stormed his place. I got there early and brought a few things home, since you never can tell. Noodles and sour herring and smoked eel and chocolate powder. Because last night I dreamed…"

Hanne couldn't describe her dream adequately, because Nesthäkchen broke in laughing: "If there's famine, then we'll dip the noodles in herring sauce and eat the smoked eel with powdered chocolate!"

"Oh, Anne, child, you are too young to understand the seriousness of the time." Hanne turned to the elderly lady, hoping to find more understanding.

Grandmother had heard quite enough. "Please call Klaus for coffee, Hanne, and see if Herr Hans is back yet." End of the entertainment.

The cook returned shortly. "Herr Hans is not yet here, and our Klaus has also gone out."

"Klaus gone also?" Grandmother had been mother to Dr. Braun's offspring for five days and was not used to the job. Whenever Klaus disappeared, she became frightened. "I thought he was reading in his room. Where can the boy be hiding now?" It wasn't easy to cope with these wild grandchildren. Grandma was accustomed to peace and quiet.

Annemarie fought with herself as she stirred her cocoa. She knew full well where brother Klaus was, since she had long been his confidante. He had gone to *Unter den Linden* with some friends, because something was always going on there.[2] Was it not Annemarie's duty to calm Grandmother, who was worried about Klaus' absence? But Annemarie did not want to tattle. What should she do?

"Extra! Extra!–great victory–fortress of Liege taken by storm" came the cry from the street as Nesthäkchen pondered her dilemma.[3]

A large crowd had gathered around the bearer of this joyous news. People were ripping the newspapers from his hands. The first big victory!

Happy people spread the word.

"Such a step forward, just a few days after the declaration of war! Anyone can see that God is on our side!" Thankfully Grandmother folded her hands.

The floor positively burned under Nesthäkchen's feet. Oh, to be downstairs among the happy tumult.

In the midst of the constantly growing knot of humanity, Annemarie's sharp eyes discovered a familiar brown curly head above a blue and white striped sailor suit.

"There is Kläuschen, just look, Grandma. He is helping to distribute the Extra edition. Oh, let me help him, please, please dear Grandma!"

Like the wind, the little girl rushed away before Grandma could object. But soon, in the teeming crowd, the elderly lady appeared in a red muslin scarf, eyes bulging behind her glasses.

In the meantime, Doctor's Nesthäkchen happily took part in disseminating news of the first victory. The newsboy was leading the parade of Berlin street youth, Klaus at the head, waving the screaming headline: Extra! Extra! Great victory at Liege!

The crowd, eyes glowing, cheeks burning, waved the headline at Grandma just as she encountered Annemarie. Should she scold her granddaughter or rejoice over the victory? In the end, she did both.

---

2. *Unter den Linden*, (Under the Lime Trees), is a broad main thoroughfare in central Berlin.

3. The Battle of Liege lasted from 5-16 August 1914. The numerically outnumbered Belgians inflicted surprisingly heavy losses on the German invasion force. The Battle of Liege was the first land battle of the war, as the German Second Army crossed the frontier into neutral Belgium to attack France from the north. With the significant aid of howitzers and the Big Bertha gun (a 420mm siege howitzer) the Germans captured the forts defending the city on 16 August. On the following day, 17 August, the German Second Army, together with First and Third Armies, embarked upon a wide sweeping wheel movement through Belgium, forcing the Belgian army back on Antwerp. Brussels itself was captured without resistance on 20 August.

Most reproaches bounced off Klaus' thick skull. But Annemarie stood glued to the spot, filled with consternation. Dear Grandmother again had reason to be angry. And Annemarie had only recently resolved never again to agitate the elderly woman.

Annemarie's bad conscience often troubled her, especially when she was rebuked. Her premonitions should have been her guide, but often they were not. Indeed, in the children's sanatorium she had the same problem.

Annemarie threw both arms around Grandmother's neck, begging and flattering. "Don't be angry, best of all grandmothers. Germany is rejoicing over the first victory. You shouldn't scold. I helped distribute copies of the Extra! edition for the Fatherland."

Could the elderly lady stay angry? You didn't have to be Grandmother to be unable to resist Nesthäkchen's pleading blue eyes.

"I'm an old lady and too weak for the wild society of you youngsters," said Grandmother finally. "It takes the strength of youth to keep you bandits in line. I will write to your former Fräulein, to see whether she would like to come back. Who knows when mommy will return?" Grandmother sighed deeply.

"Oh yes, my beloved golden Fräulein!" Annemarie's eyes glistened. The little girl had deified her Fräulein, during the many years Fräulein was a member of Dr. Braun's household. Tears flowed when Fräulein returned to her mother and Annemarie was sent to the North Sea children's sanatorium. And now Fräulein was coming back—the idea was too wonderful.

Klaus was less enthusiastic. To be forced to behave around the house was a distinctly unattractive prospect. Fräulein would limit his freedom. She had always kept him on a tight leash.

"I do not think you are so old, Grandmother," said Klaus in a courtly way. "Our high school principal is certainly older than you; he has not only white hair, but also a white beard. And he manages to control many boys who are far worse than I am." But it would have been difficult for his schoolmates to be wilder than Klaus, since in school he was their acknowledged leader.

Klaus had not convinced Grandmother. "Where is Mommy? What is she doing this long with the old English, who have all turned against us?"

The doorbell rang. "There is Mommy now—that's certainly her," said Nesthäkchen, running to the door expectantly, as she always did.

But the child returned disappointed.

Again in vain. Again the non-appearance of the fervently-awaited mother. It was only brother Hans returning, worked up, from his railroad station duty.

Today the senior high school student didn't seem tired, although since early morning he had been working at the Schlesicher Railroad Station. To the troop trains passing through, Hans had helped drag baskets with cups, pitchers of coffee and great plates of stacked rolls.

"A famous victory, yes, when we Germans finally cut loose. Good day, Grandma. Little one, how is it going?" Hans' greeting had to play second fiddle to his joy of victory.

The good grandmother had already made her grandson a refreshing glass of lemonade. "Are you very tired, my boy?"

"No, not at all. Today was something else! You, Klaus, you should have been there. Just think, at noon we Pathfinders brought slices of buttered bread to an arriving train composed of cattle cars adorned with garlands. And because our boys in field gray tried to take the bread in a mannerly way, we had a chance to talk with them. There was one who laughingly assured me that his soldier's stomach couldn't hold any more, even if he tried to eat. But I didn't give up until he finally took a slice with sausage. Then one of the other Pathfinders tapped me on the back. 'Man, don't you know who that is?' he whispered.

'No,' I said.

'That is Prince Joachim!'[4]

"And it was Prince Joachim. In the middle of the cattle car among all the others, just as though he was one of them. Was I proud that the prince ate my bread and sausage right up. And as the train pulled out he waved at me."

---

4. Joachim Franz Humbert Hohenzollern (1890-1920) was the sixth and youngest son of Kaiser Wilhelm II. Joachim held the title Prince of Prussia and served in World War I as an officer and aide-de-camp. On September 9, 1914, during the battle of the Masurian Lakes, he received a shrapnel wound of the right thigh not involving the bone. He married Marie Auguste von Anhalt in 1916; she later left him. On May 31, 1918, when much of Europe lay in rubble, the renowned psychiatrist Professor Robert Gaupp examined Joachim. Gaupp determined that the prince was mentally and physically incurably ill. Indeed, two years later, in a state of rage, Joachim killed himself with a pistol shot. Joachim spoke rapidly, Dr. Gaupp wrote, showed quick twitchings of his face, was mentally and sexually enormously excitable, and tended to vehement, avalanche-like outbreaks of fury, during which he lost self-control completely. Despite good intelligence, Joachim had a highly developed sense of self-esteem that made him act on impulse. Any impediment would cause a pathologic paroxysm of fury. Dr. Gaupp noted vasomotor disturbances marked by quick facial reddening and believed that Joachim had a genetic disease, which others have diagnosed as *porphyria*, a condition that also affected Joachim's ancestor, England's King George III (Röhl, John C.G. Wilhelm II: der Aufbau des Persönlichen Monarchie. CH Beck. Munich 2001).

Filled with joy, Hans whirled his little sister around the narrow balcony. Grandmother approached to see and hear.

In the meantime Klaus ripped a button from his brother's jacket and held it tightly. Klaus wanted to experience even more of this exciting event. "A real prince—tomorrow I'm certainly going to the Schlesicher Station. Maybe I can help there. Our Kaiser has many sons. Maybe tomorrow another prince will come through," said little Klaus with a gleam in his eye.

"Oh right. There are not princes everywhere. The luck I had comes only to the truly fortunate. And you won't be of any help, my little boy, you are no pathfinder." Hans soundly thumped his breast.

"Doesn't matter, I'm going anyway. Will you come with me, Annemarie?"

"You bet!" Nesthäkchen's blue eyes gleamed even more brightly than Klaus' brown ones.

"Out of the question. You will all stay here," said Grandmother. "There's no way I'm letting you two into that mad crowd at the station, among all the locomotives. I won't have a quiet moment unless you are both right here."

Nesthäkchen accepted her fate with a heavy heart. But the useless Klaus plotted how, despite the interdiction, he could evade the grandmotherly eye and escape the house.

In the evening, when all her grandchildren were safe in bed, Grandmother was able to breathe easily. The uproar and excitement had been too much for her. She sat down at her desk and wrote to Fräulein. She was no longer up to the difficult task of caring alone for her daughter's children, amidst the chaos of war.

Meanwhile, Nesthäkchen lay in bed and prayed with all her heart: "Dear God, let my beloved mommy come back soon to Berlin, but not the old Russians. And protect my father in the war. And also Uncle Heinrich and all the other soldiers. And send us another fine victory like today's, OK? Please help us Germans, dear God."

Nesthäkchen suddenly realized that, perhaps at this very moment, French or English children were also praying for God's help. So she quickly added, "And if you don't want to help us, then don't help the others, either. At least stay neutral, dear God. Amen!"

Figure 1. Filled with joy, Hans whirled his little sister around the narrow balcony. The building in the background is the Reichstag (parliament).

CHAPTER 3

▼

HOW THINGS LOOKED IN NESTHÄKCHEN'S SCHOOL

The window curtains across the way at the Thielens were finally raised. A little brunette girl's head appeared in the nursery window and nodded a happy greeting to Dr. Braun's daughter.

"Come onto the balcony, Margot, then we can speak more easily with one another," cried Annemarie through cupped hands, overjoyed to have her friend back.

The two friends stood on their adjacent balconies, a low wall between them. After their long separation they reached out to one another.

"Good day, *Margotchen*, I believe I'm now taller than you; my braids are certainly longer. Are you still first in your class? And do you believe that the Russians are coming to Berlin? Our Hanne says they are. My father is with the army in France, yours too? Grandmother is staying with us, and my old Fräulein will be back day after tomorrow."

The little chatterbox Annemarie hardly let her friend get in a word.

"Yes, my papa is also in the army. He volunteered for duty. Mamma and I cried so when he left," said Margot.

"My mommy is in England, among our enemies," said Nesthäkchen.

"Oh, Annemarie, is that why you're so happy?" said the astounded Margot.

"No, mommy will be back soon, perhaps today or tomorrow at the latest," replied Annemarie, with the optimism of youth.

"Did you forget me when you were in the children's sanatorium, Annemarie? You wrote to me so seldom," said Margot, a deeply thoughtful, quiet child.

"Not a bit," Annemarie said. "I had another best friend there, Gerda Eberhard from Breslau. But now you are my best friend again, *Margotchen*. Oh, I would frightfully love to kiss you." In vain the little blond girl tried to reach her dark-haired friend, but the separating wall intervened.

"Wait, *Margotchen*, I'm coming right over. We must kiss, since we haven't seen one another in more than a year."

"Wonderful—I'll open the door. But our place looks sloppy. Our trunk has just arrived and been unpacked."

"No matter, I won't come into the house."

"Then how will we meet? Outside on the steps is certainly unpleasant," said Margot bewildered.

But her bewilderment was only to increase.

"You'll see. I'll be there." A prominent rustling sound emanated from the stone tiles of the balcony. Even before Margot realized what was going on, a laughing blond head popped up above the separating wall. The wild little bumblebee had propped a table against the wall, climbed up on it, and hummed a popular Berlin melody:

> *Just look*
> *There he strides*
> *Long steps he takes*

"Nice, no?" said Nesthäkchen as she dropped down on the Thielen's side, to the amazement of her staring friend. Soon they were sitting together on a chair, after composing themselves and straightening their locks. Higgledy-piggledy they blurted out their experiences during the lost year.

"Just think, my doll Gerda drowned in the North Sea during my flight from Wittdünn. Are you in Fräulein Hering's class? Marlene Ulrich is no longer first? Are you still good friends with Ilse Hermann? And is that Hilde Rabe still so impudent?" Margot was unable to answer the questions as quickly as Annemarie could ask them.

Suddenly, in the middle of the lively girlish chatter, Grandmother's voice was audible nearby. "*Annemiechen*, darling, come along, we are going for a walk. My goodness—where has the child gone? I was sitting in the next room, and I didn't see her pass by. Merciful heaven, I hope nothing has happened." Grandmother looked anxiously up and down the street, to see if the little rascal had tumbled down.

But Nesthäkchen sat hidden behind the wall, giggling furtively like a demon. What a peculiar situation.

"*Annemie—Annemie—*" Grandmother's voice sounded more frightened than before.

"You have to tell her where you are," whispered Margot, who was a very well behaved girl.

The high-spirited Annemarie finally returned home, naturally the same way she had come. This time she had to put the chair on top of the table. As Grand-mother's cry again rang out—"*Annemiechen*, darling, where are you?—Nesthäkchen shouted, "I'm hanging right here." In a bright blue linen dress the girl rolled over the balcony wall, falling at the feet of Grandmother, who clapped her hands together in horror.

"*Annemie*, how can you act so wild? You aren't a boy. Didn't you hurt yourself, child?" Grandmother was very happy to see her granddaughter before her, safe and sound.

"No, I'm not hurt at all," said Nesthäkchen as she began to cry.

The child's crying made Grandmother more upset. She thoroughly examined her grandchild. "Where does it hurt, where? Tell me. Shall I take you to the doctor?"

"Not the doctor," said Annemarie, "the tailor." Laughing through her tears, Nesthäkchen displayed a large triangular rip in her pretty summer dress, a souvenir of her journey.

"You see, *Annemie*, what happens when you behave so unlike a girl. Now it's too late to go for a walk, if you must change your clothes.

So the first reunion of the two friends had sad consequences. But Annemarie resolved never again to be un-girl-like. How long would she keep her resolution?

Next day school began.

Five minutes before a quarter to eight, Annemarie Braun and Margot Thielen walked out their front doors simultaneously. How happy Margot was to walk to school again with her friend. Annemarie was even happier. In fact, her joy returning to school was unbounded, after having been away for a year. What would the children say to her? And Fräulein Hering, who had always been so nice to her.

The walk to school today was a thousand times more interesting than ever. The streets teemed with soldiers in field gray. Gray military cars raced by. At the railroad station troop transports came and went. The sounds of an organ emerged from the Kaiser Wilhelm Memorial Church.[1] Every morning a prayer service was held in the church for the soldiers going off to war. At the end of this war, would there be another victory?[2]

In front of a red brick building, the Schubert Girls' Lyceum, a large group of schoolchildren greeted Doctor's Nesthäkchen like a good old friend. Why didn't everyone go inside? It wasn't too early. But the group of girls hummed like bees in a hive. As the friends moved closer to one another, their excitement increased.

"Don't go in. School is over," shouted Erna Rust, a classmate, to her fellow students.

Doctor's Nesthäkchen responded "*jawohl*," but in fact did not allow herself to be led so easily. Margot went straight in, but stopped in the school courtyard, undecided what to do.

Inside, groups of excited students were standing around, conferring with one another. Among them were strange men, dragging benches and tables. Suddenly the girls began laughing boisterously. Professor Möbius, the French teacher, was carrying his lectern on his back. Was the whole world going nuts? What did all this mean?

Two of Nesthäkchen's friends, Marlene and Ilse, appeared. "Hi, Margot. Hi, *Annemie*. Good to see you back. Know what's going on?" Everybody wanted to be first to tell everyone else what was happening.

"What is this? What's the matter? Is the whole school crazy?" cried Annemarie in a disrespectful manner, meanwhile burning with curiosity.

But before Marlene or Ilse could answer, another girl, Marianne, arrived and shouted, "Our school is being converted to a military hospital. We have to move."

"What?" Margot's jaw dropped.

---

1. The architect Franz Schwechten designed the neo-romantic Kaiser Wilhelm Memorial Church, built 1891-95. The church is located on Breitscheidplatz, in central Berlin. Inside are friezes commemorating Chancellor Otto von Bismarck's three victorious wars against Denmark, Austria, and France. The building was heavily damaged in a 1943 Allied air raid. The ruin has been preserved as a war memorial. Berliners, who refer to it as "the broken tooth," say it is the only structure in town whose appearance was improved by the bombing.
2. The previous war, the Franco-Prussian war, ended in 1870 with a resounding German victory.

Annemarie let loose a flood of questions. "Are the wounded already inside? Will our teachers become nurses? Will we have no more school until the war is over?"

"Yes, cupcakes, school is moving," screamed the friends to one another. "But we don't know where."

This situation was quite interesting. None of the hundreds of students of the girls' school had ever experienced a relocation. Did you simply go home? Should you stay there? Nobody knew, and the excitement increased.

"I'm going quietly to my class. No teacher has said a word," decided the diligent Margot.

"I wouldn't do that in my dreams. It's much more fun out here in the courtyard. Besides, soon there will be soldiers inside." Doctor's Nesthäkchen beamed at the unforeseen events.

"The military hasn't arrived. First they have to empty the building," explained Marianne Davis eagerly.

"At best they'll load us all into the junk room," laughed *Ilschen* with the blond curls.

All at once, the loud voice of a teacher broke through the chattering of the girls. "Quiet—the students will assemble in the gym."

"Good that we didn't go home," said Margot, pulling her friend Annemarie into the gymnasium.

The room was packed tightly with girls, big and small, blond and brunette. The former strictly segregated classes were dispersed among each other willy nilly.

Outside, the war raged, and the different social classes, rich and poor, educated and uneducated, whirled in turmoil among one another. Inside, in the little world of the girls' school, things were no different. On the long exercise bars, bold girls from the tenth class had made themselves comfortable, despite the protests of students of the first class, who felt the bars belonged to them. Annemarie Braun had found herself an empty spot far above. In high spirits, Doctor's Nesthäkchen dangled her legs, covered with knee-length stockings. From her perch she had a good view of the crowd. Margot, who dutifully followed everyone else, was not so lucky.

A group of teachers, men and women, entered the hall. Close to Annemarie, Fräulein Hering's friendly face appeared.

"So, back again, Annemarie Braun? It's wonderful you have returned to us. You're burned as brown as a little girl-fisherman." Fräulein Hering approached and extended her hand. Annemarie reached down at the same time and—oh my—lost her balance on the narrow bar. Striving not to fall, she tried to grasp with her left hand anything nearby. She fell and caught herself with both arms around the teacher's neck. Fräulein Hering laughed heartily at this tender greeting, and Annemarie purred with pleasure.

In fact, the experience had also been somewhat embarrassing for Doctor's Nesthäkchen. Luckily the principal appeared and quickly mounted a podium built of crates and mattresses.

The principal cleared his throat but did not speak. To the great astonishment of the students, the singing teacher, Herr Lustig, in field gray uniform, sang out in his magnificent bass, "A cry rings out like a clap of thunder."[3] Brightly all the girls joined in the musical celebration.

Then the principal spoke, simply and warmly:

"My dear students. When we separated five weeks ago, to collect new strength for diligent work, we had no inkling of what a powerful storm would break over our beloved fatherland.

"The German oak is strong to its roots. Though many foreign hands try to shake it, it does not sway. Instead, it stands more steadfast, ready to splendidly bear leaves again.

"Each of you probably has a proud family member who has joined the holy struggle for Germany's freedom. Teachers from our own faculty have enlisted in the army. Some of our lady teachers have reported to the Red Cross as aides. But the war also demands sacrifice from the school itself. Our rooms are being fitted out as places of healing for the wounded. In spite of much effort, I must ask for four volunteers to help transport the heavy furniture. A few young people from the Pathfinders League have offered their assistance. But teachers and students must do most of the work. I am completely convinced how happily each of you will contribute to that cause for which others are sacrificing their lives. Students from the tenth to the sixth class should go home. Students in the middle and upper classes who wish to help should go to their classrooms and follow the

---

3. *Es braust ein Ruf wie Donnerhall...*, is the first line of the German patriotic song, *Die Wacht am Rhein*, composed by Carl Wilhelm and Max Schneckenburger in 1840. After the Nazis came to power in 1933, they mothballed this song because of its association with the lost World War. But *Die Wacht am Rhein* surfaced again in the movie *Casablanca* (1942). On account of copyright problems, Warner Bros could not use the genuine Nazi party anthem, *The Horst Wessel Song*, and so the movie Nazis sang *Die Wacht am Rhein*, which the French patriots movingly drowned out with the *Marseillaise*. No one sings *Die Wacht am Rhein* in Germany today, at least not in public.

teachers' directions. Other students can leave, since all help is voluntary. You will be notified when school will resume. Resumption depends on our finding space in another school in another part of the city. We anticipate that instruction must begin again in the afternoon. Teachers and students should accept this small inconvenience to assist the fatherland.

"Do not waste your extended vacation. You all have the duty to marshal your strengths. I therefore exhort the girl students to form a work division for the Red Cross. You will hear more about the work division later. Every class must choose three representatives, who will see that every student follows school regulations.

"And now, my dear students, before we attend to our work for the fatherland, let us give three cheers for our ever most gracious Kaiser: hooray, hooray, hooray![4]

Deeply inspired, the young girls cheered in unison the supreme commander. Hundreds of jubilant voices then rang out in the golden August day: "Hail to you in the wreath of victory."[5]

So ended the inspiring celebration.

To work! The little girls, who were of no use, looked jealously at the bigger ones. And none left. Everyone wanted to help. If there had been a little lazy-bones who wanted to go home, she would have been ashamed in front of the others.

How happy Doctor's Nesthäkchen was to be in the sixth class and able to help with the move.

Every class had a different task. One packed up maps, another carried instruments. The art room and the library had to be emptied out. All schoolbooks and other volumes were sorted and carefully packed. The assembly hall and gym served

---

4. After the war, people felt differently about their former Kaiser, Wilhelm II, whose inept rule had led to the murderous conflict. The theater critic Alfred Kerr wrote:

Was man klar an ihm erkannt
War der Mangel an Verstand.
Sonst besaß er alle Kräfte
Für die Leitung der Geschäfte.

What was clearly recognized in him
Was the lack of a mind.
Otherwise, he possessed all strengths
For the management of the businesses.

5. *Heil dir im Siegerkranz* is an 18th century patriotic song, with the same melody as *God Save the King* (or *My Country 'tis of Thee*).

as a collection point for various school paraphernalia. The teachers took off their coats and, their faces sweating like porters, dragged out tables, benches, and lecterns. Teachers and students did their work with hot cheeks. The school was like an ant colony, with everyone eagerly running about to perform her assigned task.

The new director of the sixth class was Fräulein Konrad, who instructed her girls to empty the classroom cabinet and student library, and to pack the contents into wash baskets. Amid the tumult, Ilse Hermann, a little bookworm, became engrossed in an engaging storybook. Ilse put her index fingers in her ears, and in the midst of all the commotion had not the slightest idea where she was.

Annemarie Braun, who had just dragged a stack of books nearby, gave the stack a friendly nudge. The books toppled onto the otherwise engrossed Ilse. "Hey, laziness isn't tolerated here!"

Ilse jumped up with alarm. Margot, who had been helping Annemarie collect the books, smilingly said, "Should our wounded have to wait until you have finished your story, Ilse?"

Blushing, the little bookworm went to work again.

Wow, was it hot. Annemarie's face glowed like a poker as she ran upstairs and down with her loads. But what difference did the heat make? Nobody was complaining today.

Some boys who were Pathfinders carried the tables and benches from the sixth classroom.

"Look out," the boys called to the girls rushing back into the room.

"Hänschen, my Hänschen," came the happy response. To the amusement of the students and Pathfinders, Annemarie Braun jumped on a bench that was about to be carried out and kissed a Pathfinder.

"Hänschen, how did you get here?"

Hans was very embarrassed, although he loved his little sister dearly. Deeply flushed, he squinted at his grinning comrades and said in a military way: "From the Pathfinders' League, commanded to serve." Then he proceeded to carry out the bench. But Nesthäkchen was thrilled at the unexpected encounter.

As first in the class, Margot had the honorable task of bringing out safely the large globe, which was almost as big as she was. Annemarie helped her faithfully. She stayed close to Margot and every few seconds reached out to the smooth round thing, to take it from her friend if Margot became tired. But Margot was exceptionally eager. Although her arms were growing gradually lame, she didn't want to show weakness.

Figure 2. Annemarie Braun, who had just dragged a stack of books nearby, gave the stack a friendly nudge. The books toppled onto the otherwise engrossed Ilse.

"Let go," Margot said a bit petulantly, and made an impatient gesture, after Annemarie had offered her assistance for the umpteenth time. All at once the spiteful, smooth world-ball slipped from the tired girlish arms— bum-de-bum-bum. It lay with a huge hole on the stone steps.

Horrified, Margot began to cry. Annemarie had a frightened expression on her face. Poland had been shattered and Russia had a healthy bump.

"It's all your fault, Annemarie. Why were you grabbing for the globe? You made me drop it. Oh, what will Fräulein Konrad say?" lamented Margot though her hot tears.

Annemarie stood stock-still. The unjust accusation her friend had made cut her to the quick.

"I didn't grab onto it at all. I meant well. But if you want to act this way, I'm through with you forever. From now on, Marianne Davis is my best friend," exclaimed Doctor's Nesthäkchen, her face cherry red with anger as she began to cry.

A crowd of curious onlookers quickly assembled around the two quarreling girls.

"Alright, what's going on here?" Professor Herwig, one of the oldest teachers in the lyceum, peered down over the rims of his glasses at the howling children.

"The globe fell down. Poland got a hole and Russia a bump," sobbed Annemarie. Margot was so distraught that she was unable to speak.

"That's truly a good story." The old professor reached for the damaged world globe. "Now, dry your tears," he said smiling to the crying children. "The world is going to pieces in the war, and what could be better for this world globe? Hopefully the damage will be a good omen for our army in the east. They will conquer Poland and give Russia a good bump—hahaha." He laughed loudly. A few other teachers passing by joined in.

But the two little friends were not in the mood to laugh. Margot was still crying. In tears, Doctor's Nesthäkchen picked up the damaged globe and carried it off. Margot followed, dabbing at her eyes with her handkerchief.

"Ay, children, what sort of funeral is this?" Fräulein Hering stopped the two mourners. The misfortune had touched her too.

"How did this happen, Annemarie?"

Doctor's Nesthäkchen bowed her blond head and did not reply. She was not going to tattle on her former best friend Margot. Better Fräulein Hering should discern the situation herself.

But Margot raised her brown head after a strong inner struggle. "I threw the globe down," she said softly.

"No, I'm the guilty one," Annemarie said forcefully. She would not allow herself to be less magnanimous than Margot.

"That is noble of you, children, that one does not try to betray the other. That is true friendship." Fräulein Hering walked away with a friendly expression, and did not scold the two girls for their clumsiness.

The two turned redder than red. They regarded each other uncertainly, ashamed of the praise that they truly had not earned.

Was it Annemarie, or was it Margot, who took the first step toward reconciliation? Afterwards, neither girl knew. But suddenly they grasped each other's hands, these two who were "finished forever". Above shattered Poland they exchanged a conciliatory kiss. They accepted together Fräulein Konrad's mild rebuke when their teacher saw what had happened.

It would have been terrible if so excellent an endeavor, the eager girls' readiness to help the wounded, had alienated these two friends.

CHAPTER 4

▼

FOR THE DEFENDERS OF
OUR FATHERLAND

"Many hands soon finish the work." The truth of this proverb was evident in the girls' lyceum. In barely three days, most of the moving had been done. The assembly hall and the gym were packed with objects that had been in the class-rooms. A huge kitchen was built, bathroom facilities added, and five hundred beds brought in.

Now the girls' duties began in earnest. Each received a printed announcement:

To the girls of the Schubert Girls' Lyceum of Berlin.

In these difficult days you shall be given the opportunity to occupy your-selves for the welfare of the fatherland.

The teaching staff has decided to found help-divisions of the Red Cross:

1. A knitting and sewing division (director Fräulein Hering). This division shall produce woolen stockings, gloves, bed linen, etc for our troops. Our lady teachers will oversee the work, which will be completed at home, so far as possible. As a place of instruction, Herr Director Schubert provisionally has volunteered his official resi-dence. Girls in this division shall assemble Monday, August 10th, 4 pm, in the school courtyard.

2. A catering division will be established (director Fräulein Neubert). The division will provide refreshments for troops passing through.

This patriotic activity in the service of the Red Cross requires a great deal of money. Therefore, all students are asked for monetary contributions, which will be collected by student-trustees and sent to the director.

Make sacrifices for the fatherland!

Margot sent Doctor's Nesthäkchen this announcement, despite the fact that it could be got from the chosen trustee-students, who had been assigned the task of distributing it. When Annemarie received her official copy, she sent it to Margot. Thus the two girls had mutually exchanged the same notice.

Annemarie sat deep in thought with her notice, although she already knew what it said. She had a difficult decision to make. Should she do sewing and knitting or serve food to the troops? Or should she do both?

This tomboy had no particular affinity for needlework. Finishing her first wrist warmer was for Nesthäkchen a form of torture. "Catering," that sounded much better. It made you think of tasty ham and long sausages. And she would be able to serve buttered bread and coffee to the troops passing through the railroad station, like brother Hans. She discussed the matter with Klaus, who, with his ravenous appetite, advised her to do catering. But Klaus didn't know how fond Annemarie was of Fräulein Hering, who directed the knitting and sewing section. Whereas Fräulein Neubert, well known in the school as a strict disciplinarian, directed the catering section.

Grandmother, the wisest of all, cast the deciding vote.

"Grandma, where shall I report? I've done enough knitting with you. Margot and my other friends are knitting in the afternoon. But I like the idea of catering much better. It will definitely be more fun." Nesthäkchen looked expectantly at the elderly lady.

"Darling, don't you know what I will advise you to do?" Grandmother laughed her charming laugh.

Annemarie squinted with one eye, which she often did when she was thinking of mischief. "Naturally I know that old ladies are always in favor of sewing and knitting. Klaus likes eating. And you, Grandmother, have said that it makes no difference how you serve the fatherland, as long as you do something.

Silently Grandmother pointed with her finger to a line in the announcement.

"Make sacrifices for the fatherland," read Nesthäkchen.

"Yes, to be sure, I will gladly do that, Grandma. I will write to Father and ask if I may donate my bank savings book. Perhaps you have gray wool or linen left over that we can bring along, and Hanne will surely give me a sausage."

The girl regarded her grandmother proudly. She had nothing else to sacrifice.

But Grandmother shook her head.

No child, money and objects alone are not enough. To sacrifice is to give something that is difficult to give. We must give our time and our work to the fatherland. Don't think only of having fun. Think of what will help our soldiers most. Now, darling, which section will you join?

"I have to think about it first, Grandma." Annemarie wrinkled her forehead as she pondered. "Food is as essential as clothing for our boys in field gray. But you know, Grandma, I'll join both sections.

"That's not a good idea, *Annemiechen*. Better to do one thing completely than many things by half.

Annemarie was spared the necessity of making a decision. Margot arrived to work with Annemarie on a list of things to collect, and told her that only older students in the first and second classes would be able to join the catering division.

As a consequence, the next day Annemarie Braun found herself with hundreds of other girls in the school courtyard, reporting for her work detail.

The girls were divided into twenty groups, and were to get together on different days of the week. Many of the teachers made their homes available for the knitting and sewing groups.

How happy Annemarie was to have joined the knitting group, because the meeting days were among the most agreeable of the week.

The bold Berlin sparrows, who regarded the principal's garden as their private property, were very surprised. Every day they saw blond and brunette girlish heads among the trees and bushes, as a hundred girls attended eagerly to their work.

What didn't the industrious girls make? Stockings above all, because "our soldiers cannot march barefoot to Paris and Petersburg," Fräulein Hering joked. Such words spurred the children to even more eagerness.

But Fräulein Hering's words were not necessary. The girls were already anxious to do everything possible for the fatherland's defenders. A noble competition began among them to see who could finish her work first. They were constantly watching each other to determine who was ahead of whom. The knitting needles clattered ceaselessly, and the talking even more ceaselessly, as chatter was also part of the noble competition.

It was noteworthy that Doctor's Nesthäkchen, who had never particularly cared for knitting, was working away on a long stocking. The stocking grew and grew. Grandmother could hardly believe her eyes. But the adult advisers and the competitive work transformed the knitting to a different task than it had been at home. Annemarie strove ceaselessly not to fall behind, even during the hottest days when beads of sweat glistened on her forehead. Fräulein Hering praised Annemarie, who, when she returned home in the evening, also enjoyed Grandmother's astonishment.

Annemarie's industry did not cease at home. Grandmother had to make sure that the child went for her daily walk. For Annemarie was determined that Margot, Marianne, Ilse, and Marlene should not finish their stocking before she did. The five friends all had their place beneath the towering nut tree, and peeped among themselves just as the sparrows did above.

More beautiful than the work itself was the girls' tireless singing. Patriotic songs and soldiers' songs rang out in the principal's garden at all hours. The unmusical sparrows had to keep their beaks closed.

Above, on the railroad bridge that bordered the garden, military trains rolled by one after another with inspired, waving soldiers in field gray. The diligent group of girls waved back with ardor.

How the principal's quiet garden had been transformed. And if an Extra! edition of the newspaper announced another German victory, the rejoicing never stopped.

Unforgettable days, these splendid August days, as German troops surged forward victoriously, and the people at home pitched in to help in any way they could. All of the young children working for the fatherland were having a soulful experience that would stay with them their entire lives.

Even Klaus, who initially lamented that his school had also not been converted to a military hospital, so that his summer vacation could be prolonged. Klaus was reconciled when he saw that much was being learned in German schools during these August days that had never been learned before.

The learning was not book knowledge. The teachers imparted to their students something else: passionate love of the fatherland, unlimited sacrifice for the fighting men, and ennobling pride to be a German boy or German girl. Despite the difficult times, each child had to fulfill his or her increasing duties.

But what was the reason that Doctor's Nesthäkchen, enthralled by these August days, often cried into her pillow at night? During the day the happy girl, more uninhibited than any of her friends, sang and leaped through the house like a weasel. No one noticed that something was amiss in her young soul.

No, no one knew what troubled Nesthäkchen. Only the moon knew for certain. The moon was Annemarie's good old friend. Year after year his caresses streamed through the nursery window and he stroked her cheeks with his silver fingers.

Nesthäkchen longed for mommy's goodnight kiss.

In the first days after her return, Annemarie was not terribly upset at her mother's absence. The war enchantment affecting everyone was stronger than all other emotions and effectively suppressed them. Then came the reunion with Father followed shortly by his departure. Annemarie's brothers welcomed her, and she became quite attached to Grandmother. And mommy must come back soon; surely she had only been delayed. So Nesthäkchen hoped from day to day. But time passed and mommy did not appear.

Annemarie had spent a year in the children's sanatorium with hardly a pang of homesickness. Now that she was at home she began to long for her mother. But not during the day. When novel events drowned out everything, Annemarie's thoughts were elsewhere. Only at night did she miss mommy.

To be sure, Grandmother came faithfully to her bed and kissed her grand-daughter tenderly. But she said, "Good night, my darling," or "my dear heart." Mother and Father had said "Goodnight, my *Lotte*." How Nesthäkchen longed for these two words, a nickname from her earliest years. Yet when Father wrote in his letters to Grandma to say hello to "his *Lotte*," it wasn't the same as when mommy took Annemarie in her arms.

There wasn't any word of mommy. Not a line had she written, despite the many letters Annemarie had sent her. In England among Germany's enemies, had Mother forgotten her daughter completely?

At first, Annemarie had asked Grandmother, then badgered her, why mommy didn't care any longer about Annemarie. But when Annemarie noticed that the question made Grandmother sad and brought tears to her eyes, she stopped asking. Why distress the good Grandmother?

Annemarie turned to her brothers. Hans, the eldest, calmed the little girl. Maybe all the letters were at the border and not let in to the enemy's country. This was a very plausible explanation.

But Klaus had mixed up war and assorted crime stories he had read. His impressions had a less tranquilizing effect on his sister. "Listen, Annemarie, our enemies have certainly captured Mommy. They have locked her up in a dark cas-tle dungeon, without even bread and water. When I grow up, I will travel to England and liberate Mommy. You won't recognize her, though. Grief will have turned her hair white."

Nesthäkchen had terror in her eyes. Hans laughed. "Boy, don't deceive the lit-tle girl. Mother is surely with aunt and uncle on their estate enjoying English roast beef."

"And if in her stone dungeon she doesn't get bread and water, she will have starved long before you have grown up, Klaus," Annemarie replied curtly.

Klaus' horror story made a deep impression on the little girl. At dinner she put down her fork. The food stuck in her throat, despite the fact that it was her favorite dish, hash brown potatoes with stewed fruit.

"Darling, don't you feel well," said Grandmother fearfully.

"No, no, I can't eat any more," said Nesthäkchen, beginning to cry for no apparent reason.

The tears of the usually happy girl were more remarkable than her loss of appetite. Grandmother was right to worry. She prodded and pressed but got no answer other than, "I feel fine and I can't eat anything else."

In the absence of the parents, Grandmother took her responsibility for her grandchildren quite seriously. She decided to telephone the doctor, her son-in-law's stand-in, and ask him to visit Annemarie that evening.

The doctor came. Grandmother led him to Annemarie's bed, since the girl had already gone to sleep. Her face, streaming with tears, was buried in her pillow.

"Doctor, the child is sick; certainly she hurts someplace. Why should she be crying? She is such a cheerful girl." Grandmother had turned pale with agitation.

"We will soon see. Now tell me, my child, where does it hurt?" Nesthäkchen was accustomed to being treated by her father when she was ill. She shook her blond head. She was ashamed that the strange doctor saw that she had been crying.

Meantime, the doctor began to examine her. But after tapping, listening, and feeling, he found nothing despite his best efforts. The girl was healthy through and through.

"What signs of illness have you noted, gracious lady?"

"The child won't eat and she cries."

"Has she been feverish? Has she vomited?"

Grandmother shook her head. No, that wasn't the case.

"I advise that the child stay in bed tomorrow. Perhaps a childhood illness will develop. Light diet, take her temperature three times a day, watch for chills," directed the doctor.

To Nesthäkchen the doctor was over-reacting. Why should she stay in bed when she was in perfect health? Why shouldn't she go to the knitting hour of her beloved Fräulein Hering? She couldn't countenance Margot and her other friends finishing their stockings before she did. Moreover, Fräulein was arriving, and Nesthäkchen was determined to meet her at the train. For this she should stay in bed? No, better to triumph over her shyness and announce why she was crying.

"I'm not a bit sick, doctor. I haven't eaten anything at all because—because—" Here Annemarie hesitated.

"Why then, my child?" said the doctor cheerfully, trying to help elicit the problem.

"Because my mommy must starve in England, without even bread and water." The words tumbled out along with a sob.

"How do you know this, darling? Have you received any word?" Now poor Grandmother began to fret over her far-off daughter.

"No—Klaus told me."

Grandmother breathed a sigh of relief.

"Klaus is a dumb boy to say such a thing, and you are an equally dumb girl to believe him. My profound apology, doctor, that I bothered such a busy man for nothing." The elderly lady was truly pained.

The doctor smiled as he calmed her.

"I'm happy that my visit was for nothing, and that the daughter of my dear colleague is completely healthy. Don't worry about your mother, my child. The English don't treat ladies so severely, even if they are citizens of an enemy country. Say hello to your father for me in your next letter. If your brother Klaus tells you any more stories, believe only half of what you hear." The friendly doctor nodded to Annemarie in a kindly way and said goodbye to Grandmother.

Annemarie's stocking was finished the next day. Of course, Marianne discovered that the sock was more suited to an elephant foot than a soldier's foot. But she was also jealous that she had not gotten so far.

Toward evening Annemarie waited with Klaus at the railroad station to meet the dear Fräulein, who had cared so many years for them.

Fräulein could hardly recognize Nesthäkchen. How the girl had grown in a year. She was almost as tall as Fräulein herself. How strong and red-cheeked the pale little thing had become, a true joy.

In the Braun home Fräulein had even more opportunity to marvel at the change in Doctor's Nesthäkchen. How orderly the nursery looked. Fräulein always had to clean it up. The shoeboxes and cabinets were in good order. Naturally, before Fräulein's arrival, Annemarie had rearranged the disorderly storage spaces.

Nesthäkchen had become a self-taught lady's aide during the previous weeks. Grandmother was old and couldn't do much. Hanne took care of food and drink, but knew nothing of embellishing a table with a flower vase. Annemarie, however, had learned these skills in the children's sanatorium. She brought the footrest to Grandmother, and cleaned the crumbs from the table after meals, although no one asked her to do so.

The pleasant reunion with Brother Hans surprised Fräulein. The Great World War had terminated the earlier nursery war that had raged between the two. Amidst war, peace reigned among Dr. Braun's offspring.

Fräulein was most amazed when Annemarie displayed, with the pride of an artist, the first stocking she had knitted. Fräulein would never have credited the tomboy with such persistence. My goodness, what war had wrought!

"When I finish the second stocking, I will crochet earmuffs for our soldiers, and trusses, and head protectors. We don't have any school at all, Fräulein, only handwork with Fräulein Hering, because our school has become a military hospital. And the older students have formed a catering division. They cook soup with the principal, and they prepare buttered bread for the soldiers. And my pocket money, Fräulein, I have put in our accounts for the Red Cross. Margot, Ilse, and I have been chosen student trustees for our class. We collect the money, bacon, sausage, and wool too. Grandmother and Hanne have already given me quite a bit."

"Ay, *Annemiechen*, I should give something too." The good Fräulein took from her trunk some packages of woolen yarn, which she handed to Annemarie for the cause.

"Thank you, a thousand thanks, my dear, golden Fräulein. I have one more request. I must whisper it in your ear."

"What can it be?"

"I would like to address you as *du*, as I did before, Fräulein," whispered Nesthäkchen.[1]

"That goes without saying, *Annemie*," said Fräulein laughingly. She hadn't noticed that the girl had avoided using the second person.

Annemarie's joy at Fräulein's return was unbounded. She hadn't been sure whether or not using *du* would offend Fräulein. Now, the nights without Mommy wouldn't be so disagreeable, because Fräulein would be sleeping next to her in her room.

Almost everyone in the house was happy at Fräulein's return. Grandmother felt that a heavy load of responsibility for the children had been lifted. Hanne

---

1. There are two ways to say *you* in German. *Du* is the familiar (second person) form of address. The polite form is *Sie*. In other words, Nesthäkchen is saying that she wants to be on the same familiar terms with Fräulein that she had been as a small child.

thought: "If the Russians do come to Berlin, at least there will be one more female here to fight them off."

Hans saw in Fräulein someone to take care of ripped off buttons and torn stitches, which he didn't always bring to Grandmother. Only Klaus and the dog Puck had forebodings. Both had gone their own way during the first weeks of the war. Puck had made himself at home on various sofas in the house; the usual occupants were absent and Grandmother did not always notice. But Fräulein would take Puck to task. Klaus had similar concerns, as he was only too eager to escape into the street. Both perceived in Fräulein's presence the end of their golden days of freedom.

CHAPTER 5

▼

NESTHÄKCHEN PUNISHES JAPAN

Fräulein's first job in Doctor Braun's house was the sewing of flags. There was already a huge finished black-white-red family flag. Also, each of the children had his or her own flag. Hans painted his with the Prussian eagle. Klaus made his in the Austrian colors, black and yellow, so that it could be seen from the street.

So many flags were needed because the splendid August days of the iron year 1914 brought victory after victory. All Berlin was a sea of waving, billowing flags. At Longwy, Namur, and Maubeuge the Belgians, French, and English felt the German fist. German submarines sailed boldly forth to the east coast of England.

How proud Nesthäkchen was, when she told her big brothers that at Wittdünn she had seen a submarine. How the boys listened, when Annemarie described the narrow black iron cigar with its small conning tower and periscope, which the sea suddenly appeared to swallow up. Afterward, the submarine could travel many hours underwater.

One day, when Klaus brought home a newspaper extra edition, "Heroic deed of the *Königen Luise*," Annemarie's excitement was unbounded. This boat, on which she had sailed from Hamburg to the Island of Amrum, had been so brave. Certainly her friend, the sailor Willem, who had shown her the whole ship, had been one of the boldest. She would send the earmuffs, which she had just finished, to him in gratitude. To be sure, the earmuffs had an undeniable resemblance to two gray mice because Annemarie had pulled the wool too tight, but the sailor would love them nonetheless.

Annemarie bought pipe tobacco with her pocket money. Grandmother added a pair of stockings and a flask of cognac, the brothers chocolate, and Fräulein a head protector. Even Hanne had to part with an attractive Rügenwalder sausage as a result of Nesthäkchen's ceaseless begging. This splendid package, and the letter Annemarie wrote the brave sailor Willem, would have made him very happy—if he had received them. Alas, he got neither Annemarie's gray ear mice, nor anything else in the beautiful bundle. Sailor Willem was already sleeping his eternal sleep on the ocean floor.

While Doctor's Nesthäkchen hung her *Königen Luise* banner to wave from the balcony, and the flowered paneling in the nursery was being proudly adorned with paper *Königen Luise* flags, the magnificent new steamer was torpedoed on a patrol, and though she fought valiantly, went down with her entire crew. [1]

Annemarie wept hot tears when she learned the fate of the *Königen Luise* and her friend. War had seemed to her a very happy event, with all the banners and victory celebrations. Now Doctor's Nesthäkchen saw for the first time the seriousness of war.

How did things look in Wittdünn, which lay amidst the sea? Had all her good friends remained there? From Helgoland, the bulwark against England's sea power, cannons were certainly firing. Mommy had spoken of these guns when she left.

Annemarie sent the school custodian Piefke, fighting at Mulhouse, the returned package with a new letter. This time the package reached its intended recipient. Piefke wrote a thank you note on the first field postcard.

Japan joined Germany's enemies. Nesthäkchen decided to avenge herself on this traitor.

In her apartment building, high up in a small rented room, lived a gentleman whom the children called the "Japanese," in spite of the fact that he was Siamese. [2] Annemarie had taken an immediate interest in his foreign appearance. This pleased the gentleman, and he developed a friendly relationship with the little blond girl whom he met on the stairs, who stared at him so curiously. Annemarie

1. British destroyers sank the German auxiliary minelayer *Königen Luise* in the North Sea, August 5, 1914.
2. Siam changed its name to Thailand in 1939, changed it back to Siam in 1945, and on May 11, 1949 officially became Thailand.

curtseyed to him. And the narrow-eyed gentleman gave foreign stamps to the two brothers and chocolate bars to the sweet-toothed girl.

But now that the Japanese man was one of Germany's enemies, Nesthäkchen determined never to greet the "Japanese" again.

One day, when she returned from her knitting hour, she met the "Japanese" by chance on the stairs. He had no inkling of Annemarie's hostility. He didn't notice that the blond girl crouched almost to the floor to avoid greeting him. He didn't even notice the absence of the friendly curtsey, which was difficult for a polite girl like Annemarie to avoid. He passed by her with an amiable, "so, have you been diligent?"

Nesthäkchen thought she had triumphed. "I really showed that Japanese man my contempt. To me he's air," she said proudly to her friend Margot.

"My mommy said that we children must greet everyone in the building in a friendly way; otherwise we are impolite," said the well-behaved Margot.

"That's nonsense. Being impolite to our enemies is patriotic," Annemarie bristled.

Fräulein had a chance to discuss the matter with Annemarie before she went to bed. Rudeness was never patriotic, said Fräulein, no matter whether it was directed at friend or foe. To be impolite was simply a sign of poor upbringing.

Her brothers also did not approve of Annemarie's behavior. "All the Japanese have gone," said Hans.

"They must have forgotten one," retorted his sister.

"I find Mr. Japanese to be very nice," said Klaus.

"Sure, because he's always giving you stamps. You'll never catch me betraying Germany for a few stamps," said Nesthäkchen with blazing eyes.

Annemarie was true to her word. She never looked at her former friend. She grimaced if he tried to joke with her, and ran away as though she had an enemy army at her heels.

One day, rushing down the stairs, which she loved to do, Nesthäkchen encountered the man.

"So, little one, don't we know each other any longer?" asked the gentleman in a friendly way with his hand on her blond braids.

"No," blurted out Annemarie, angrily trying to escape.

"We must renew our acquaintance," said the unsuspecting "Japanese," shoving a piece of chocolate into the child's open mouth.

"I don't take gifts from our enemies," said Nesthäkchen, spitting out the chocolate on the red-carpeted staircase. Before the gentleman appreciated the meaning of the clearly rude gesture, Annemarie tore herself away.

Figure 3. "So, little one, don't we know each other any longer?" asked the gentleman in a friendly way.

No, Doctor's Nesthäkchen would engage in no traitorous act, although the chocolate was delicious.

Annemarie proceeded to avoid the "Japanese," with the painful feeling she had behaved very crudely toward him. She told no one about her heroic deed, except for Margot, her best friend. Margot was so horrified that Doctor's ashamed Nesthäkchen began using only the back stairs.

One day, Annemarie met her neighbor unexpectedly. She was in the middle of the *Tiergarten*,[3] together with Klaus who was feeding goldfish in the pond. Grandmother was sitting on a bench.

Klaus raised his cap when he recognized the man. Annemarie turned her head away, half defiant, half embarrassed.

"Where is the curtsey, Annemarie?" asked the foreign man standing before her. By this time he knew the girl's attitude toward him. With a smile he added, "You can look at me calmly. I'm not Japanese, I'm Siamese."

Oh, how ashamed was Doctor's Nesthäkchen. She would have liked to crawl into a mouse hole. She secretly regretted not having eaten the tasty chocolate, because after her first unpleasant confrontation she received no more.

---

3. A large park in Berlin

CHAPTER 6

▼

A LITTLE GIRL PATRIOT

School began August 24. Not in the old rooms, to be sure, which were already filled with wounded soldiers. A *Volksschule* nearby allowed the Schubert Girls' Lyceum to share space.[1]

Instruction for the girls could begin only in the afternoon, since the morning was reserved for the *Volksschule* students. This arrangement was disagreeable both for the teachers and the students because instruction did not begin until 2 PM. In many families mealtimes had to be changed and other household routines were disrupted. But on account of the wounded, the families made the necessary sacrifices without complaint.

Not Dr. Braun's Hanne, who cursed and grumbled. Her workload was increased, since she had to prepare a separate meal for Annemarie. Yet it wasn't the increased work that annoyed Hanne; rather it was the fact that "her child" couldn't have a peaceful noon meal. The food appeared punctually on the table, but Nesthäkchen was an excitable little thing. Pre-school agitation disrupted her appetite, and if Fräulein or Grandmother were not there, half the food remained on the plate.

---

1. A *Volksschule* is a German school providing only basic primary and secondary education, inferior to that of a lyceum or *Gymnasium*, which prepare students for university.

Everything in school was different, not only the classrooms but also the instruction. Many teachers had answered the call to arms, among them the principal. Old Professor Herwig reluctantly assumed direction of the school.

It wasn't always easy to rule the little female empire. Apart from the difficulties of the changed schedule, the war and the long summer vacation had profoundly affected the girls. They had to accustom themselves to school in the afternoon. At first they were not serious about their studies. Among the blond and brunette braids was talk of the thunder of the guns, the trenches, longing, postcards from the front and extra editions of the newspapers. Little mental energy was left over for the subjunctive and irregular verbs.

In the *Volksschule* many girls did not thrive.

"I'm ashamed to death," said Ilse Hermann to her friends after the first day of school. "Hildegard von Meissen from the Girls' *Gymnasium* lives over there. What if she thinks I'm attending a district school?

"Nonsense, you're not going to a district school; we're only visiting," said Marianne.

"Anyway, children from the district school aren't worse than us," said Marlene.

"Yes, in the trenches rich and poor are fighting next to one another," said the perceptive Margot.

"Our Kaiser said, 'there are no more parties.' That means all men are now equal," said Marlene.

Annemarie, otherwise the liveliest of the group, was silent today. She blushed and pretended to be looking at pitchers of milk and white cheese in a dairy store nearby, although she had no particular interest in dairy products.

Annemarie friends' words disturbed her. She found it painful to have classes in the *Volksschule*. Around the corner was Klaus' *Gymnasium*. What if his friends thought she was a district school student?

But Marlene had shown Annemarie how dumb and arrogant she was. From now on she would not think she was any better than the poorer children.

Next day, during the recess before French class, Doctor's Nesthäkchen again opened her big mouth.

"No, I won't study more French. Why should I torture myself with irregular verbs? I'm too full of love for the fatherland," said Annemarie forcefully.[2]

---

2. Very few German students today learn French. In the Heilwig Gymnasium (high school) in Hamburg, English is the required foreign language. Twelve of the 690 students, almost all girls, study French. The one boy in the group, age eighteen, said that he risked heckling from the other boys. Some of them thought he was a sissy for choosing French. (Tagliaube, John. For France and Germany, still no love lost. New York Times. March 14, 2003 A3.)

"Annemarie, French is an immutable part of the curriculum. You must learn it," said Margot in a reasoned way.

"To me it's a lot of chirping. I can do without it," retorted the blond girl.

"We don't want French class either," said Marlene. "We love the fatherland as much as you do."

"No, no, German girls will not learn French," chimed in the entire class in wild tumult.

"Alright, what ungodly noise is this?" said Professor Möbius, the French teacher, wrinkling his forehead at the girls.

Deep silence.

None of the pupils uttered a peep. All of them buried their noses in their despised French grammar books.

But Annemarie was not afraid. A German girl was no coward. She stepped forward with a defiant air.

"Doctor, I ask you to allow me to dispense with French class," she said loudly.

A clap of thunder! The other students stared with wonder at the bold girl. Their courage, which had disappeared when confronted with the Professor's wrinkled forehead, surged anew.

Professor Möbius peered at the girls as though they were not right in the head. "Are you sick?"

"Not at all. I am a German girl. I will not learn the language of our enemies," said Annemarie, spiritedly tossing back her blond pigtails.

"We won't either. We don't want French class," rang out the cry from small courageous groups.

Marlene and Ilse stepped forward to place themselves alongside Annemarie.

The teacher's serious face took on a wry expression. He looked at the rebellious females and was secretly pleased at their inspired love for the fatherland, though they had expressed it in a childish way.

"So you don't want French class. Great. Do you think you're helping Germany to defeat France one hour sooner?" he asked quietly.

The girls were silent.

"Is it going to do our fatherland or our bold troops any good if you don't learn French?" asked the teacher.

The students looked trumped. Canceled French class would do nobody any good, especially not the girls themselves, though the irregular verbs would not continue to torture them.

"On the contrary, you will be hurting the fatherland and yourselves," said the teacher gravely. "I see you children don't believe me. Germany needs educated young people. In these great times our strength must not fail. Hopefully the war will not last long. When peace comes, there will again be intellectual and commercial relations among many peoples. Think of the consequences if German girls don't learn French and English. None will be able to take the examination to become teachers. None can work in international commerce, because French and English correspondence is a vital part of this work. The fatherland will be deprived of these strengths. You will be inadequately educated for many professions, because language instruction is part of your education. You won't enjoy your acquaintance with foreign countries because you won't understand what people are saying. Anyone who loves the fatherland will demonstrate her love by being doubly diligent and eager." Thus spoke the intelligent teacher as he opened his French grammar book.

The excited girls recognized their foolishness. They proceeded to make exceptional efforts to show love for the fatherland through industry and ambition.

Annemarie Braun became friendly again with the "disgusting" irregular verbs. But on the way home she couldn't restrain herself from expressing her convictions to her friends. "When our boys in field gray defeat France, everyone there will be speaking German, and we will have learned French for nothing." This time she didn't generate much enthusiasm. The professor's incisive words were ringing in the girls' ears.

His comments generated interest in Ilse's suggestion to put a foreign word box in the classroom. Every contribution of a word not mentioned during class would be rewarded with five pennies. The money would be used to buy Christmas presents for men confined to the military hospital that had been the girls' lyceum. A foreign word box would also be kept at home, the money to be dispensed to any charitable cause the donor desired.

"That's great. Grandma is always saying *adieu*. Now she'll have to contribute five pennies every time she says it. And Aunt Albertinchen uses one foreign word after another. I think all old people like to do that. If only Aunt Albertinchen will come soon," said Annemarie hopefully.

No one in the house was safe from Nesthäkchen. She was like a police dog that would not let a foreign word escape. She soon filled her box, which had been given to her by a friendly home guard in field gray. After one lunch she was fifty pennies richer.

"Hanne, leave the leftover soup in the *terrine*," said Grandmother.

"Hurrah, five pennies," shouted Nesthäkchen, terrifying Grandmother. "It's called soup bowl."

Hanne brought the roast.

"The cream sauce for the *roast beef* is turned out quite well." The old cook was hardly able to get out the words.

"Hanne, a groschen—half for *sauce*, because a good German says *Tunke*—and the other half for *roast beef*. The correct word is *Rinderbraten*," shrieked Annemarie.

"What—?" exclaimed an agitated Hanne, with her red hands on her wide hips. "A little child is telling me that this isn't roast beef? I've been a cook for twenty years. I can certainly tell roast beef from *Rinderbraten*. And you're calling my delicious cream sauce *Tunke*?" It took a long time for Hanne to calm down. She didn't give a thought to the fact that the fine she had to pay would go to the men in field gray.

The others had to pay, too, despite the Fräulein's wariness: "You won't catch me, *Annemiechen*."

Klaus recounted glowingly that he had made only two errors in his math *Extemporal*. His extraordinary diligence cost him half a groschen. He asserted that no girl could understand that the *Gymnasium* word was *Extemporal*. But Hans agreed with his sister. Even in *Gymnasium* one could write *class work*.

"OK, pull out your *Portemonnaie* and pay up, my son," said Hans laughingly.

You too, you too, *Hänschen*," said Annemarie, happily clapping her hands. "We say wallet, not *Portemonnaie*. Exuberantly she sprang from the table, although the meal was not over.

"Annemarie, first lay down your *serviette*," called Fräulein after the tomboy.

"No, Fräulein, I certainly won't lay down my *serviette*, but I will put down my napkin." Nesthäkchen sat down, laughing as she looked at Fräulein's dissatisfied demeanor. "You see, beloved Fräulein, now I've caught you, too."

Grandmother had to pay the most to the foreign word collection box.

At her advanced age, did she have to unlearn everything she had learned? No one should be asked to do that. She arranged flowers in a *vase*, as she had always done, not in the flower-container her patriotic little grandchild demanded. She lowered the *Jalousie* on the sunny balcony, even when the diminutive know-it-all insisted on the Venetian blinds. And the *chaiselongue* on which Grandmother took a nap after meals: the elderly lady would never call this piece of furniture a deck chair, despite Nesthäkchen's best efforts.

When Aunt Albertinchen, with her gray bun, appeared in the afternoon, Grandmother acquired someone to share her sufferings.

"I ran into Klaus with his *botany* drum. Is he taking a *landpartie*?" said Aunt after greeting everyone.

Nesthäkchen patriotically pounced on her old aunt. "Aha, Aunt Albertinchen, you must pay a groschen into my foreign word box. *Landpartie*—phooey! *Excursion* is the proper word, also *plant drum*."

The good lady had no idea what was wrong, and her eyes showed surprise.

"The child has been torturing me all day with her foreign word antipathy. I'm worn out," laughed Grandmother.

Nesthäkchen also laughed, with the world's most mischievous face.

"Antipathy, Grandma? OK, you're pardoned. You don't have to pay any more today. You've already shelled out a frightful sum," said the grandchild sympathetically.

Grandmother wanted no "pardon" and consequently had to pay another ten pennies.

Aunt Albertinchen laughed so heartily that her gray locks appeared to be laughing with her. "Ay, get my *pompadour*, my darling, it's next to my *mantille*, so I can pay the fine."

"*Pompadour*—bag!" trumpeted Nesthäkchen. The sensitive Aunt Albertinchen recoiled fearfully. "And *mantille* is certainly a foreign word. One can say *cape* just as well."

"Let me see if the *kondukteur* gave me enough small change." Again Aunt Albertinchen was in for a shock. The piece of chocolate that she took from her bag and gave to Nesthäkchen was not enough to placate her.

"You know, darling, you can get me something from Lemke. Fräulein knows about it." Grandmother made a dismissive gesture toward the girl. As much as she loved Nesthäkchen, today the child was getting on her nerves.

Lemke was a pastry baker and Konditorei proprietor next door.[3] Nesthäkchen had no objection to visiting him.

"I want six *Eisbaisers, Annemiechen*." Fräulein gave the child some money.

"Certainly, *Eisbaisers*, give me half a groschen for my box. I'll get *ice kisses*, Fräulein," said the tomboy as she ran out.

The chubby konditorei proprietor was astounded when the child asked for six *ice kisses*.

"Ice kisses? Mr. Lemke stroked his bald head. "Oh, you must mean chocolate kisses?" and brought out the tray.

"No, no, *ice kisses*," replied Annemarie, who saw at once that the man had no idea what she was talking about. Giving up, she added, "I mean the former *Eisbaisers*."

---

3. A *Konditorei* is a café and bakery.

"They're still called that," replied the puzzled baker, finally bringing her what she wanted.

As Annemarie left the shop with her ice kisses, the newspaper boy on the corner was calling out with an Extra! edition in his hand.

Hello—had there been a new victory? Love for the fatherland and dreams of another day with no school lent wings to Nesthäkchen's feet.

"Hindenburg's big victory at Tannenberg, more than 30,000 Russian prisoners!"[4] A car had stopped at the corner. A jubilant crowd was grasping for copies of the victory report fluttering from the car.

Annemarie got hold of a paper and took off at a gallop. She wanted to be the first to spread the happy news at home, and to be able to hang out the victory banners before her brothers did.

Despite her hurry, Annemarie had to study the terse report. No wonder that she gave no thought to holding her *ice kisses* upright. As a result, the *sauce*, no the *Tunke,* from the strawberry ice cream splattered her bright blue linen dress.

But what was the harm, in the face of such a magnificent victory, which seemed to be more meaningful than the first report indicated? Hindenburg had hunted down the Russian army in the Masurian swamps.[5] How could this achievement be compared to Aunt Albertinchen's deathly shock, when Nesthäkchen raced onto the balcony howling like an Indian: "Extra edition! Extra edition! Big victory at Tannenberg!"

And what could anyone say when Annemarie herself had to pay five pennies to the soldiers in field gray? She had shouted *Extra* Edition, rather than *Sonderblatt*! But the little girl patriot was happy. Wasn't her victory banner the first on the entire street, though innumerable brightly colored banners were soon fluttering in the wind? And all the bells of Berlin were chiming out Hindenburg's mighty victory.

---

4. The most spectacular and complete German victory of the First World War, the encirclement and destruction of the Russian Second Army in late August 1914 virtually ended Russia's invasion of East Prussia when it had hardly started.
5. Colonel General Max Hoffmann (1868-1927) planned the Battle of Tannenberg. But at the time, Field Marshal Paul von Hindenburg (1847-1934) got the credit. When Hoffmann later took visitors over the field of Tannenberg, he would tell them, "This is where the Field Marshal slept before the battle; here is where he slept after the battle; here is where he slept during the battle!" (Tuchman, Barbara. The Guns of August. Macmillan. New York 1962.)

CHAPTER 7

▼

NESTHÄKCHEN HELPS THE EAST PRUSSIAN REFUGEES

The Field Marshall's splendid victory eliminated the frightful, menacing Russian danger that had threatened verdant East Prussia. But Hindenburg was unable to help the poor people that the thieving, marauding, murderous Cossacks had driven from house and home. Others had to provide this aid.

Endless lines of refugees flooded into the large cities. Every day trains packed with people fleeing East Prussia arrived at the *Schlesicher* Train Station in Berlin. The passengers were a heavy burden for the volunteers there. The number of Pathfinders almost doubled to be able to accommodate them. The young helpers had been excused from school, because an afternoon shift at the station was not enough.

When Hans Braun came home exhausted each night from the station, he described the misery he had seen throughout the day. The long trains were disgorging hordes of pathetic human beings, forced from their homeland and their peaceful activities, carrying their worldly possessions in bundles. People, goats, and chickens were jammed into cattle cars. Some were in mourning after Cossacks had murdered or abducted beloved family members. Parents were wailing for their children and children crying futilely for their parents—a sad, sad picture that appeared every day before the Pathfinders' youthful eyes

But their ability to help the suffering stimulated feelings of exultation in the young people's souls. After his day's work, despite all the agony he witnessed, Hans had a sense of inner satisfaction, which comes only to a person selflessly assisting others. For a high school student, this satisfaction was at least a small consolation for not being able to join the army and go to the battlefield, which Hans dearly wanted to do.

The compassionate Grandmother's eyes filled with tears when she heard about the sufferings of the refugees. She helped however she could.

Klaus and Annemarie took in the situation with interest and curiosity. Like other children, they wanted to get involved in the adventure. Klaus gave his last groschen to the East Prussians, instead of using it to buy a snack. Nesthäkchen donated the money in her foreign word chest to the pathetic refugees.

Like the Zeppelins that were bombing Antwerp, the little sister and brother bombarded their big brother with questions.

"Tell me, Hans, what do the Pathfinders do in the new refugee reception area that was built at the station?" Klaus asked, filled with secret envy for his brother's work.

"With a Red Cross nurse, we take down the refugees' names, their previous addresses, and their intended destinations."

"But are you curious where they're actually going?"

"Every day we get inquiries from refugees' families about whether their relative has passed through Berlin. We Pathfinders need to know this so that we can provide information. During the tumult of their flight in the overfilled trains, many family members are separated from one another. They come to us for information about the location of their loved ones. Many of the people have relatives in Berlin and we Pathfinders must show them the way. The average East Prussian farmer has never left his town and immediately becomes lost in Berlin. We take the refugees from one train station to another if they are traveling further. Sometimes we call their relatives in the city, who might want to visit with them during their short stay. We bring the homeless to shelters. We give donated food to the hungry and distribute clothing that has been contributed.

"The suffering we see is horrible. Often the people don't have coats on their backs. In fear of the Cossacks, parents have pulled children out of bed in their nightshirts and they are not dressed properly until they arrive here. We must try to contend with these problems. The Pathfinder is like a supportive woman for everyone." The senior high school student laughed at his little analogy, despite the profound effect on him of the misery he had witnessed.

Grandma cast her eyes down sadly. How much human happiness this unholy war had destroyed. If only it would soon end victoriously.

Klaus listened with a gleam in his eye—how he envied Hans. In two years he would be able to join the Pathfinder's League. If only the war would last that long. Thus the insightful wishes of the aged stood in apposition to youthful stupidity.

Nesthäkchen left the room quietly. She didn't want her big brother to see the tears in her eyes. She always cried when she was teased. But even Klaus had behaved admirably and had left his little sister alone. The tears were a reaction to the unaccustomed tragedy.

Fräulein called to the girl.

"*Annemie*, you didn't finish your meal. You haven't eaten your egg or your ham or buttered bread. What's the matter?"

Nesthäkchen quickly dried her tears and came back to the dining room. She gazed at the table laden with good things to eat. Even though Klaus' ever-ravenous stomach had done quite a job, many East Prussian children could get fat on the leftovers.

"Fräulein, I can't eat another bite. I've had enough," lamented Annemarie. Then she turned to Grandmother, who had so often shown her kind heart. "Dearest, only Grandma, can't I give the rest of my evening meal to Hans to feed the hungry East Prussians? I ate so much at lunch. And the poor refugee children should not have to starve and freeze."

The two grown women sobbed, though they did not want the child to see their tears. The softhearted blond girl embraced the white-haired grandmother.

Neither of the two brothers, who were sitting nearby, laughed at Nesthäkchen today. Klaus patted her back affectionately and shoved his buttered bread, from which he had already eaten the ham, boldly and decisively to his older brother.

"There, you can take my food with you tomorrow." Despite his dumb pranks, Klaus was a good boy at heart.

Grandmother consoled her little loved one. "Eat my darling, your two pieces of buttered bread are not going to do anything for the hungry refugee children. You're trying to accomplish too much. Tomorrow we'll pack a basket with bread, butter, a few sausages and ham. That will help much more. Hanne will bring it to the *Schlesischer* Train Station.

"I'll take it myself. It's no disgrace to carry a basket for the fatherland," said Hans. The smallest package had previously been a burden to him, since he thought that the work of a porter was an affront to his manhood. Now he freely volunteered for such work. Thus the war educated the young.

"And we'll send laundry and clothing for the poor children, so that they don't have to run around in their nightshirts and freeze," said the sobbing Annemarie.

"Yes my child, tomorrow we'll check everything. Now eat."

"*Check* is a foreign word." Even in tears Annemarie was going to collect from Grandmother for the soldiers in field gray. Finally the girl began to eat.

Later when she lay in bed, she could not fall asleep. This time Annemarie wasn't thinking of her father in the war or the unknown fate of her far-off mommy. No, thoughts about the East Prussians driven from their homes kept Nesthäkchen awake.

How many refugee children had no bed in which to stretch their weary limbs? Was Annemarie better than those children only because her circumstances were so much better? Was she sufficiently grateful for her luck? Did she accept as her due a lovely room, a warm bed, food and clothing? Wasn't all the love that she received from her parents self-explanatory? At least until the moment they vanished from home.

These portentous, serious thoughts filled the tomboy's head, replacing all kinds of stupidities ordinarily to be found there. Even the moon, her good old friend, was amazed.

What an astonished face the full moon made when he saw his little chum silently leave her room. She sneaked up to the door and listened for Fräulein, who would have chased her back to bed. Was Doctor's Nesthäkchen up to no good?

No, the moon didn't need to make such an ugly face. Annemarie was doing nothing naughty. By the silver moonlight she went through all her clothes, deciding which she could dispose of for the benefit of the refugee children. Otherwise she would have no peace. Hans would take the clothing to the station early next morning, so that the children would not be forced to freeze for another day.

First Annemarie opened her white cupboard, in which her best clothes were stacked, festively tied with bright blue ribbons. Oh, how many shirts and stockings she had; she could give almost all of them away. Hanne, who always treated her so well, would gladly wash her clothes more often. So she didn't need more than two shirts and two pairs of stockings. The same went for her bodices, embroidered skirts, and aprons.

Annemarie tossed everything into the large white doll wagon, after she had thrown out the former occupants. The dolls, shocked out of their nightly repose, made unpleasant faces.

For herself, the child kept only two pieces of each type of clothing, which she returned to her cupboard. Then she opened her clothes closet. Now the selection process became incomparably more difficult.

The red muslin dress with the white polka dots was her school dress. She could donate that, no problem. The bright blue linen dress flecked with strawberry ice cream brought back memories of Hindenburg's victory. She was ashamed that the East Prussian children might discover her sloppiness. Maybe better to give them the pink flowered dress. "Oh, no, no, Mommy sewed that dress herself. I can never give it away," Nesthäkchen said loudly to herself.

The blue-white striped dress? That one could go. Ditto the white sailor suit, which she wore only on Sunday.

The elegant embroidered dresses were totally unnecessary. She always hated wearing them. She had to be so careful about not wrinkling the fabric. The wide silk sashes could go with them.

Annemarie tossed her green plaid dress and sailor suit into the wagon. The bright blue sash, which Fräulein had carefully wrapped in tissue paper, followed. If not, the East Prussian children would think that she had no sashes.

The little refugees needed hats and coats, too. But Nesthäkchen could not bear to part with her beloved sailor cap. It was so wonderfully comfortable, and she could toss it wherever she wanted.

The varnished black hat she could get rid of willingly. The white Florentine hat with its wreath of wildflowers she preferred to keep. Her friend Margot had the same one, and when the two wore their hats together they looked like twins. Annemarie preferred to donate the elegant pointed hat Grandmother had given her, since it was impermissible to stretch it or sit on it.

There was not a large selection of coats. She would have preferred to keep the sailor jacket with its brass buttons, but, oh, the freezing children needed it more than she did. The sports jacket was altogether too small for her.

It was autumn, and the days were sometimes quite cool. All right, she would simply wear a winter coat. Certainly it wouldn't make her sweat.

Oh, heavens, she had almost forgotten the boots. The poor little refugees would have to run around barefoot.

She was especially attached to her sandals and would never give them away. But the rest of her footwear, the white, brown, and black shoes and boots, landed right on top of the delicate pointed hat, which no one was supposed to sit on, and on the blue sash, which Fräulein had so carefully wrapped in tissue paper.

The doll wagon was stacked with Nesthäkchen's most beautiful things. On the floor nearby lay piles of clothing that would not fit into the wagon. After a satisfied glance at her work, illuminated by the silver moonlight, Nesthäkchen crept back into bed. With a beatific smile on her lips, she quickly fell asleep.

Fräulein was not amused when she entered the nursery one hour later. What had the tot done here?

She had pulled her best things out of her closets. The carefully folded embroidered clothes were bunched up under the boots. The pointed hat—the apple of Grandmother's eye—lay on the floor.

Angrily Fräulein began to bring order to this scene of chaos. She had no idea of Annemarie's motivation, and thought the child was being naughty. Early tomorrow morning Fräulein would have a few sharp words for her ward.

But when Fräulein discovered the piles of underwear, she slapped herself on the forehead. Of course, why hadn't she thought of it before? Annemarie had obviously done everything for the East Prussian children. How could anyone scold her for that? With a good, compassionate heart, the uncomprehending little girl had selected things she wanted the poor children to have.

Annemarie continued to sleep peacefully. While she dreamt of seeing the East Prussian children wearing her finest Sunday clothes, the clothing itself, one piece after the next, was migrating back into the depths of the closets. The moon giggled into his palm.

Next morning, anxious whispering awakened Fräulein from a deep sleep.

"Fräulein, dear Fräulein, wake up," rang the excited voice from Nesthäkchen's bed. "We were robbed last night."

The horrified Fräulein sprang from her bed, flailing with every limb. "What? What's the matter? Did you hear or see anyone, Annemie. We must call the police immediately. Is anything valuable missing?"

"Nothing, Fräulein." Nesthäkchen did not dare to speak loudly. The thieves might still be in the house. "But we've definitely been robbed. The thieves took all my underwear and clothing that I wanted to give to the East Prussians."

Fräulein shot the little girl a puzzled look, then laughed out loud.

Had fear caused Fräulein to lose her mind? Something was sure to happen if the burglars overheard.

"Child—Annemie—what a dummy you are to frighten me so. Last night I put back all the lovely clothing that you ripped from your closets. Now it's where it belongs. Don't go throwing all your things around again." Fräulein had stopped laughing.

"The clothes were for the refugee children." Nesthäkchen breathed more easily, since she now knew that no thief had paid her a visit.

"Really, Annemie, what will the impoverished children do with your embroidered dresses, sashes, and white hats? Such things are totally impractical for them. They have no Hanne to wash and iron."

The little girl was not convinced. "They can use the underwear and boots. You can let me give those away, Fräulein."

"Annemiechen, you need the underwear and boots yourself," said Fräulein with a yawn as she crawled back into bed.

"To give away what you don't need anymore, that's not proper. Grandma says only that which is dear to you has any value. We must learn to make sacrifices." As Nesthäkchen philosophized, Fräulein snored contentedly.

Grandmother decided that her granddaughter had been too generous. Grandmother herself, along with Fräulein, selected clothing from all three siblings, a respectable basket full. Although pointed hats and silk sashes weren't included, the East Prussian children would value the warm woolens and felt boots more highly. On top of the pile Annemarie placed a toy. After all, the poor children with no homeland were entitled to a little fun.

CHAPTER 8

▼

A LIVING DOLL

It was Sedan Day, that great day, the foundation of Germany's fame.[1] In the schools, celebrations began before noon. The pupils of the Schubert Girls' Lyceum held joint festivities with the female Volksschule students. Poor and rich sat intermingled in the brightly festooned school auditorium. But none of the "high-born daughters" had feelings of superiority, and none of the Volksschule girls were envious of the more elegantly coifed lyceum girls. The same ennobling thought united everyone. Fame and victory, signified by Sedan Day, would come again to the dear fatherland.

Berlin was clothed in colorful flags. During the free afternoon, Annemarie wanted to walk with Klaus along *Unter den Linden*. The beautiful Berlin streets, running from the Brandenburg Gate to the old Kaisers' Palace, were the scenes of

---

1. Following a series of military defeats and blunders, just six weeks after the commencement of the Franco-Prussian war, the right flank of the French army was defeated at the battle of Sedan. Led by Emperor Napoleon III, the 83,000 strong French army surrendered to the Prussian army on September 2, 1870. Two days later, the republic of France was proclaimed. Napoleon and his staff were kept prisoner in Wilhelmshöhe (near Cassel), in a castle of the Prussian kings, from September 5, 1870 to March 19, 1871. After this resounding, humiliating debacle, a new French government was created in place of the Second Empire.

patriotic parades and martial music. From the palace windows and balcony, the younger royal princes showed themselves to the throng.

Klaus had a date with two friends. Annemarie was keen to go along.

But Grandmother was fearful. She didn't want to entrust Nesthäkchen to the wild young boys, to brave the massive crowds on *Unter den Linden*. And Fräulein had left to attend the birthday party of an acquaintance.

Grandmother had important things to do. She wanted to visit the Dutch consulate, to find out how best to send a letter through neutral Holland to reach her daughter in England.

The newspapers carried stories about riots and violence against Germans in London. The police were forced to take them into custody to assure their safety. The newspaper stories were responsible for increasing the elderly lady's worries about her daughter, from whom she had still heard nothing. She hid the newspapers from the children. Why should they too have to worry about mommy? Only the oldest, Hans, shared Grandmother's anxiety. The Red Cross had advised him to send a letter via Holland. Grandmother did not want to delay this letter for another day.

Grandmother wanted Nesthäkchen to accompany her to the consulate, but the child didn't want to. If she couldn't stroll along *Unter den Linden*, she would stay home.

So on this glorious Sedan Day, Annemarie sat alone on the balcony, knitting a truss for Father, who was quite busy, somewhere between Rheims and Verdun. But the girl got no pleasure from her work. She was the light of her father's life, yet she was unable to knit happy thoughts into the truss.

The dear sun above had a similar problem. She sent down her joyful, proud rays to the little knitting girl, but was unable to brighten her pretty young face.

Annemarie was angry, mostly at herself. Why was she so willful? Why didn't she go with Grandmother? Now she had to sit by herself at home on Sedan Day. Her friend Margot, whose society she craved, was apparently not home. Their mutual friendship signal, three knocks on the balcony wall, elicited no response.

Stupid that Hans was on duty today. Grandmother surely could have entrusted Nesthäkchen to her big brother.

Was that the front door? It could only be Hans.

Wonderful—today he got off early. Maybe the two of them could go to *Unter den Linden*.

Hans went looking through all the rooms. "Isn't there one dame in this house?"

"Yes, here's one," cried Nesthäkchen from the balcony.

"Oh, you," blurted Hans, who appeared to be in a great hurry. "Have you seen Grandmother or Fräulein?"

Annemarie was silent. She didn't like the way Hans had treated her.

"My goodness, girl, don't be so obstinate. This is important. Can't you see? At least Hanne must be around someplace."

"No, she has gone shopping. Grandma and Fräulein went out." Annemarie overcame her fit of pique because matters of importance stimulated her interest.

"Well that's a fine kettle of fish," replied the agitated Hans.

"What's wrong, *Hänschen*, you can tell me. I'm eleven years old, you know," said the girl, burning with curiosity.

"I've brought you something," said Hans, revealing a thick package hidden under his loden cape. A soft meowing sound was audible.

"Oh, a kitty, a young cat. I've always wanted one. Give her to me, Hans, please, please." Beaming, Annemarie jumped at her brother. Her bad mood was forgotten.

"The kitty is—a little East Prussian child!" Hans finally revealed the contents of the bundle, which he held awkwardly under his cape.

Nesthäkchen stood glued to the spot.

A bright red bald head was visible, along with two energetically gesticulating tiny hands, like those of an oversized doll.

"Isn't that sweet," said the astounded girl. "He's a thousand times cuter than a kitty. Are you giving him to me, *Hänschen*?" Nesthäkchen grasped lovingly at the screeching bundle. "A genuine babe-in-arms. Oh, will my friends be jealous." As she once had done with her doll Gerda, Nesthäkchen began maternally rocking the red-checkered bundle back and forth.

The crying infant became silent. Two wide blue eyes looked up in silent amazement at the equally blue eyes of Annemarie, who gazed back, enchanted.

"Don't drop him, Annemie," said Hans, wiping sweat from his forehead. It was great to be a Pathfinder. But to be a nanny, too, was a bit stressful.

"What do I do now?" Annemarie sat down, still holding the crying infant carefully. "Look, he already knows me. Surely he thinks that I'm his mother and you're his father." This thought caused Annemarie to laugh loudly.

The mortal in her arms did not seem to have much of a sense of humor. In his short life, he had had many experiences that were not funny at all. Or had Annemarie's loud laughter frightened him? He opened his mouth to cry, and a new concert began—much louder than before, and less melodic.

Annemarie stood up and began to rock the child again, but without effect.

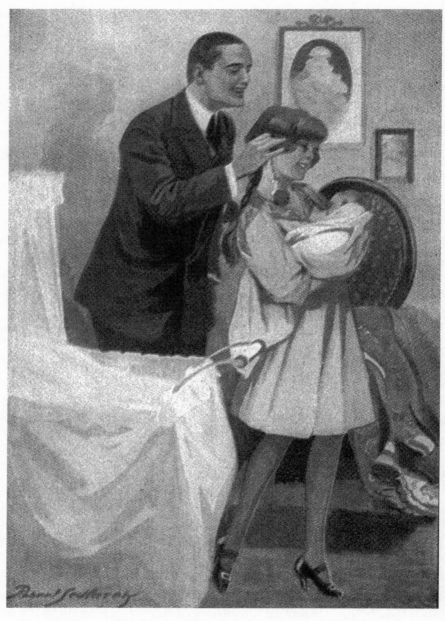

Figure 4. As she once had done with her doll Gerda, Nesthäkchen began maternally rocking the red-checkered bundle back and forth.

An amazed Hans looked at his little sister. Surely a girl was more conversant with these matters than he, especially a small girl like Nesthäkchen. Annemarie had something very maternal about her as she tried to calm the shrieking infant.

The babe-in-arms had paused in his screaming in order to collect his strength. Annemarie, meanwhile, was increasingly curious about the origins of the living doll that had suddenly appeared in the house. "Doesn't he have parents?"

"Only heaven knows," said Hans, shifting his shoulder. "East Prussian refugees picked up the worm on an embankment somewhere and brought him to Berlin. Whether his parents lost him during all the tumult, or whether they're even alive—nobody knows. We don't know his name or place of birth, either. I tried to leave him at a foundling home, but they were full. I went from one crib to another. There was no room. I finally got fed up and brought the worm home with me. We have enough space and milk for such a tiny little thing. We lack nothing.

"It's great that you brought him, Hänschen. I will raise him," said Nesthäkchen in all seriousness. "He's so small. The poor child doesn't know his parents and probably never will." Tears of compassion welled up in Nesthäkchen's eyes. Again she had witnessed the fearful suffering war had brought. And to think she was crying every night because Father and Mother weren't home. Didn't she have sufficient reason to thank God when she looked at the little worm without parents being shuffled from one place to another?

The child must have felt some inner compassion, too, because he began shouting, "eh, eh, eh."

"I think he's hungry." The noisy bundle puzzled Nesthäkchen. "Here, take him for a minute, Hänschen. I'll get him something to eat."

"Better put him on the sofa." Hans had had enough of playing nursemaid.

"No, don't do that. He might fall off. But you know, Hans, he would do famously in my doll wagon." This inspiration had almost caused the tomboy to jump for joy into the air, infant in arms. Luckily, the baby emitted an angry shriek that caused Nesthäkchen to hold him more tightly.

Hans was forced to take on fatherly duties. He had to rock the child to and fro. Annemarie proceeded to toss her dolls out of the wagon. Lolo, Mariannchen, Kurt, Irenchen, and the rest didn't mean a thing to her any more.

Truly, the diminutive guest was quite comfortable in the doll wagon. He had never had such agreeable accommodations in his entire life. The white pillows with their pointed corners and the bright blue silk tablecloth filled him with wonder and inhibited his crying.

Hans pulled the infant back and forth, from the living room to the dining room, from the dining room to the nursery. This activity was much less taxing than carrying the child around and rocking him. Hans was already exhausted.

In the meantime, Nesthäkchen laid out what she thought "her child" would be able to eat. Previous experience with the dolls was a help. They got grass-spinach and roasted pebbles. Annemarie understood, of course, that this fare was not appropriate for a living doll. Nor were the leftovers from lunch, peas and sauerkraut. She didn't like milk herself, so why should the babe-in-arms feel any different? No matter—little children must drink milk, and she was determined to give her child a proper upbringing.

Influenced by these thoughts, Nesthäkchen poured milk in a glass and returned quickly to the living room, whence the "eh, eh, eh" meow was emanating.

"So, my wee one, drink well." Annemarie held the glass to the mouth of the child, who was barely six weeks old. Naturally, he had no idea what to do, since he had always drunk from a bottle. With his tiny fist he nearly knocked the glass out of Annemarie's hand. The contents spilled over the child and the doll bed.

The babe-in-arms screamed more loudly than before and his face turned beet red. He didn't like his milk-bath.

"You are a rude little thing." Annemarie was discovering that it was not simple to raise a child. In vain she blotted the milk drops and the infant's tears with her handkerchief. What was she going to do with this howling doll?

"Should we put sugar in the milk, Hans?" Puzzled, Nesthäkchen stood on one side of the wagon, and Hans, equally perplexed, on the other.

Indeed, children cause worries.

"The glass is too big for his mouth. Maybe you should feed him the milk with a teaspoon," suggested Hans.

"No, better from my doll glass, the pretty pink one with the golden flowers. Certainly he'll drink from that."

Annemarie got the glass, poured in milk, and filled it to overflowing with sugar. The child was uncooperative. Annemarie tried force.

Whether the six-week-old infant sensed the intentions of his pint-sized foster mother, or whether the lovely pink glass drew him in, he began eagerly slurping and swallowing.

Wasn't he adorable? Annemarie beamed with motherly pride, and Hans breathed more easily. They were finally able to do something for the worm.

After the infant had emptied the doll glass five times, Annemarie believed that she had provided enough food for the moment. "Otherwise you'll spoil your stomach, child."

The babe-in-arms had the opposite opinion. He was enjoying the food, after having almost starved. But since he was not able to articulate his thoughts in grammatical German, he emitted piercing shrieks.

The foster mother was no wiser than before. Did this baby have a screw loose? Nesthäkchen had only her own experience to draw on. And she had to win the love of her child, no matter how much effort it took.

Annemarie brought her chair alongside the doll wagon, took up her knitting, and peacefully allowed the infant to scream.

"What's his name, Hans?"

"No idea. The people who found him didn't know."

"Then I must baptize him." Annemarie devoted intense mental effort to coming up with an especially elegant name for her babe-in-arms. "What do you think of *Brutus*? What about *Odysseus*? Wait, I have it. We'll name him *Hindenburg*."

Hans wanted to interject that *Hindenburg* was not a proper first name, but little *Hindenburg* shrieked him down with the voice of a field marshal.

The cook appeared in the door. She had returned from shopping and was attracted by the peculiar sounds.

"Good heavens, what have we here?"

"A sweet child. We have got a child, Hanne. His name is *Hindenburg*." The girl looked hopefully at Hanne's strong red face. What would the old cook say?

She said nothing. She tapped her forehead with incomprehension. Had the war driven the entire world crazy?

"I was afraid that the Russians were coming. Instead we get this tiny, skinny worm. Hindenburg. My goodness, how can adults give their child such a crazy name," said Hanne, with a sly look on her face.

Hans and Annemarie laughed.

"I named him Hindenburg because he has no parents and because he is my child." Annemarie screamed out this reply, but the child's shrieks drowned her out.

"Your child? Let's wait until your dear Grandmother comes home."

"Grandmother will be very happy with my child, Fräulein too, just like I am. You have no heart, Hanne. You must pity this poor lost East Prussian child. Shh! Shh! Be quiet, Hindenburg. What a powerful throat in such a tiny thing." Annemarie banged and shook the wagon. Hindenburg continued to scream angrily.

"Aw, come to me, baby," said the cook as she picked up the crying child. She certainly didn't want to be thought of as heartless. "The worm is hungry." The hunger was obvious. "He's sucking his fingers."

"That's impossible. He's already had so much milk," said the foster mother. By rights Hindenburg should have quieted down. But he hadn't. With undiminished lung power, he began to trumpet anew. At the same time, he stuck his finger in his mouth and nearly choked.

"Hindenburgchen—be careful. Tomorrow I want to take you for a walk." Annemarie's promise was without effect. She got a little ball and held it out to the babe-in-arms, but he did not know enough to reach for it.

Annemarie rang the cowbell, in use as a table bell, to cheer the infant up. Hindenburg drowned out the ringing with his screams.

Grandmother came home. On the threshold she heard the ear-splitting duet. Heavens, was this din coming from her home?

"Hanne, what's wrong here?"

"Look inside, gracious lady. You're in for a surprise," said Hanne with suppressed mirth.

Grandmother was truly surprised. Was the surprise pleasant? We shall see.

Amidst the fearful racket and her efforts to quiet Hindenburg, Annemarie noticed Grandmother, who stopped, horrified, in the middle of the room. She couldn't believe her eyes.

A living being screamed and moaned in Nesthäkchen's doll wagon, which heretofore had held only silent, uncomplaining dolls. And with her bell Nesthäkchen was increasing the clamor. Hans stood on the other side of the wagon, swinging his pocket watch back and forth, with no noticeable effect of the bawling infant.

"So, children, what does all this mean? Would you like to explain it to me?" It took Grandmother a while to make herself understood.

Annemarie spoke in her loudest voice, but Hindenburg's screams didn't help.

"Dearest, only Grandmommy, you've gotten a great grandchild." Nesthäkchen ran to Grandmother and led her to the doll wagon.

"Whaaat?" More the startled grandmother was unable to verbalize.

"Isn't he sweet? If only he wouldn't scream so much."

Grandmother shared this passionate wish. During the five minutes she had been home, the racket had addled her brain. And "sweet" was not a word she would have used, even euphemistically, to describe the beet-red bald head. How on earth did he get here?

Grandmother turned her inquisitive eyes to Hans. She had looked in the right place.

"I brought him, Grandma," said Hans a bit hesitantly, "because the poor little boy had no place to go." Hans was uncertain how Grandmother would react to the pint-sized noisemaker.

"Hans gave him to me as a gift," said Annemarie. "He has no parents. I am going to raise him. Look at your great grandmother, Hindenburg."

"What? What's his name?"

"Hindenburg. That's the name I've given him to honor General von Hindenburg," said Nesthäkchen proudly.

Grandmother started laughing and couldn't stop. "Little Hindenburg is going to live with us?"

"At least until we can find someplace else, or until his parents turn up," said Hans unenthusiastically.

"No, until he's grown up. I won't give him away. Grandma, you've always had compassion for the poor East Prussians. My Hindenburg is an East Prussian refugee. He doesn't know his parents, not at all. Can't he stay with us?" As Nesthäkchen pleaded, Hindenburg dampened his energetic screaming, as though he sensed that his fate hung in the balance.

Grandmother sank into a comfortable chair. Her vision of the future had shaken her. It wasn't enough that she had to control the wild Klaus and the willful Nesthäkchen. A shrieking babe-in-arms was all she needed.

Hans recounted the life history of the interloper, in so far as he knew it.

Grandmother's soft heart could not turn against the innocent worm, whom war had torn from his caring parents. She took the child in her arms and danced in her grandmotherly way. Hindenburg contorted his face into a pained smile.

Nesthäkchen thought she had won the game, since Grandmother was being so nice to "her" child. "Can we keep him, Grandma, can we? I will knit diapers for him and little shirts."

"Who will wash the diapers, darling?"

"Hanne would love to do that, isn't that so, Hanne?" said Nesthäkchen as she turned to the cook, who was setting the table for dinner.

"I wouldn't dream of doing it. You'll do the wash yourself, if you please, should you bring a babe-in-arms into the house," laughed Hanne. But Nesthäkchen thought that Hanne was joking.

Grandmother had now expended enough tenderness on her new "great grandchild." She laid him down in the wagon.

Hindenburg was definitely not pleased. He screamed as though he had been stabbed and sucked all his fingers at the same time.

"The child is frightfully hungry," said Grandmother. Not for nothing had she raised three children and six grandchildren. She knew immediately what was wrong.

"He has already drunk five doll glasses full of milk," said the foster mother.

"Five whole doll glasses. The *baby* is right to cry," laughed Grandmother.

"If you please. *Baby* is an English word. We Germans say babe-in-arms." On account of her new great grandchild, Grandmother had to deposit five pennies in the foreign word box.

"Dash over to the glass store next door. They have baby bottles. Buy some rubber nipples, too, Annemie," said Grandmother.

Nesthäkchen ran as fast as she could.

Returning, she met her friend Margot, who was coming home from a walk.

"Look what I have here, Margot," said Annemarie, as she displayed the baby bottles.

"So are you still nursing from the bottle?" laughed Margot.

"Not at all. I got a gift, a babe-in-arms, a cute little thing named Hindenburg."

"A doll, right?"

"No, a living doll, alive and kicking."

"Come on, you're pulling my leg," said Margot with disbelief. Who could blame her?

"If you please, come with me and take a look at my little Hindenburg," replied Annemarie, dragging her friend along with her.

Outside the apartment Margot could hear the melodic voice of Annemarie's babe-in-arms. Inside, a true living doll lay in the doll wagon.

"Is he really yours, or is he just visiting?" asked Margot.

"He's mine. Hänschen gave him to me, because the infant has lost his parents. Now I will bring him up," said Nesthäkchen grandly.

Margot left speechless and amazed.

Hanne warmed some milk and brought Hindenburg a bottle.

"I want to give him the milk, Grandma, please let me. Otherwise he won't know I'm his foster mother," pleaded Annemarie.

Grandmother smilingly nodded and placed the child in Annemarie's arms. Expectantly, Annemarie put the nipple in Hindenburg's mouth. The infant grasped for the bottle more hopefully than he had for the doll glass.

The famished infant began to suck on the bottle, once, twice, before throwing it down angrily and screaming for the doll glass. Nesthäkchen tried to put the nipple back in Hindenburg's mouth, but he resisted her efforts energetically.

"Grandma, oh, dear Grandma, come here right away," the little mother shouted toward the adjoining room. "The child is certainly sick. He doesn't want to drink anything. If only Father weren't at the front."

Grandmother tried to feed Hindenburg, but with no more success than Annemarie. As the elderly lady struggled with the baby, beads of sweat appeared on her forehead.

Klaus returned home with Puck. Both were struck dumb.

"What kind of hideous foolishness is this?" said Klaus, plugging his ears.

"You are hideous, not my sweet child," retorted the anguished little mother in high dudgeon.

"What is this disgusting screamer doing here?" Klaus hadn't a clue.

"This is your new nephew Hindenburg. He is a poor, lost East Prussian child," said Annemarie.

"What? He's going to stay here?" Klaus was unable to summon up tender avuncular feelings for his new nephew. "Who will be able to stop this murderous din?" Klaus plugged his ears even more determinedly.

"Be serious, sometimes you make a much bigger racket," yelled Nesthäkchen with injured maternal pride.

Hans carried Puck, frightened by Hindenburg's screams, out of the room. Truly, the noise was intolerable.

"I've got it. I've finally figured out what went wrong," said Grandmother, weakened by her exertions. "Hanne didn't punch a hole in the rubber nipple. The baby could have sucked all day and not swallowed a drop of milk."

Grandmother quickly rectified the mistake. The babe-in-arms joyously consumed the milk in the bottle. Nesthäkchen watched him pensively.

Hindenburg, exhausted from thrashing about, sated and happy, lay back in the doll wagon. A beneficent quiet again reigned. And all the family members had better feelings toward the new arrival.

Only Puck was unable to befriend the tiny stranger. With a low growl he circled the doll wagon.

Grandmother, too, had misgivings and shook her head. Every few minutes during supper, Annemarie jumped up to look behind the white drapes, where Hindenburg slept soundly.

When Nesthäkchen went to sleep, the doll wagon with the baby had to be next to her bed, as it had been before with her favorite doll, Gerda.

Fräulein was not expected until late that night. Annemarie wrote her a letter explaining the presence of the sleeping Hindenburg. She left the letter on the table in the nursery, where Fräulein would surely find it.

When Fräulein returned from her birthday celebration, the whole house was asleep. To avoid waking Annemarie, Fräulein did not turn on the light. As a consequence, she did not see Annemarie's note, describing who was now sharing the nursery.

It was the middle of the night. A soft, moaning *ehh, ehh* was audible. Neither Fräulein nor Annemarie noticed. Both slept soundly.

The *ehh* became louder and more demanding.

Fräulein dreamed that a herd of goats passing by her was making the moaning *eeh*, which she in fact was hearing.

Suddenly the modest groans became loud screams.

Fräulein jumped up alarmed. "Annemiechen, child, is something wrong, or were you screaming in your sleep?"

"No, it's nothing," came the drowsy voice from Annemarie's bed. "It's only Hindenburg."

"Who?" Fräulein thought Annemarie had fever and was delirious. Terrified, she turned on the light.

With blinking eyes, Annemarie looked calmly at Fräulein, as the screaming continued. Mercy, weren't the shrieks coming from the doll wagon?

Fräulein was, all in all, a courageous person, but fear had made her hair stand on end. All the midnight spook stories she had ever heard came back to her in an instant. Dumbfounded she pointed her index finger at the white wagon, the source of the loud noises. Was something there bewitched?

"He's hungry again. But the middle of the night is not the right time for a meal," said Annemarie, yawning like a lion. She was too tired for her mother-love to emerge.

"Who? Who are you talking about, Annemiechen? Your dolls?"

"No, I'm talking about Hindenburg," said Nesthäkchen, trying to stop her ears with the corners of the sheet.

The Russian troops in the Masurian swamps could not have been more frightened of Hindenburg than the poor Fräulein. Had Annemarie lost her mind? Fräulein thought. Or had Fräulein herself imbibed too much punch from the birthday bowl? Was this apparition her own fault?

Luckily for Fräulein, Grandmother appeared at the door in her purple dressing gown with Hanne in her pink night jacket.

Grandmother sighed. "This can't go on. Things can't stay like this."

To Fräulein's astonishment, the cook approached the bewitched doll wagon. When Hanne lifted a living babe-in-arms from the wagon, Fräulein's amazement was immense.

Grandmother explained the infant's presence. Fräulein became somewhat calmer.

Not Hindenburg. He screamed until dawn. He had set an entire army in motion: Grandmother, Hanne, Fräulein, Annemarie, and Hans. To curb Hindenburg's martial strivings, they tried everything in vain: rocking, riding, humming, clucking their tongues, and singing. They were weak; Hindenburg was strong. At her wits' end, toward morning Grandmother brought Hindenburg his bottle. He became peaceful, and for a short time there was an armistice.

Only Klaus and Puck slept through the night.

Next morning, the defeated held a council of war.

"I won't have Hindenburg in the house another day," said Grandmother. "I'm an old woman and can part with my sleep. But for you young children, your nightly rest is essential. I can't allow a disturbance like this."

"He'll get better. I'll educate him," said a fatigued Nesthäkchen, who with shadows around her eyes took the side of her child. But she didn't sound as lively or convinced as she had yesterday. The nocturnal concert had cooled her ardor.

"He is a born screamer. He'll never change," said Fräulein convincingly.

"He's a poor little East Prussian child, who's been tossed every which way. Who else will take him in?" Hans, who had caused the whole problem, sought to prevail, though his conscience had pained him throughout the restless night.

"I can only hope Hindenburg will find other accommodations," said the formerly softhearted Grandmother, who was now impervious to Hans' pleas.

"Take him back where you found him," said Klaus arrogantly.

"Keep quiet. You slept through the whole night." The brothers would have come to blows, had Hanne not said, "The wife of the porter in our building. She would love to have this baby. A year ago her little son Mäxchen died. Her husband is at the front."

"That's a wonderful idea, Hanne," said Grandmother overjoyed. "I'll speak with the porter's wife. She's a proper, reliable woman, and we can still keep an eye on the infant."

Grandmother promised the lady a monthly stipend for Hindenburg, and she took him gladly. Thus was the East Prussian refugee's lifeboat directed into another port. He moved into the porter's apartment and was renamed *Mäxchen*.

Nesthäkchen was secretly pleased with the way things had turned out. It wasn't so simple to mother such a living doll.

CHAPTER 9

▼

THE YOUNG GIRLS' HELPERS SOCIETY

Outside of Germany war raged in the east and west. But the Germans themselves were strongly determined to heal the wounds of battle and ameliorate the sufferings war had brought. The enthusiastic young gave gifts of love to the troops and worked for their welfare in other ways.

The girls of the Schubert Lyceum had organized themselves into a young helpers' society. Doctor Braun's Nesthäkchen provided the impetus for the organization. The society required considerably more from her than had the doctor's foster-grandson-for-a-day.

The whole sixth class knew the story of little Hindenburg. All of the children were intensely interested in the tiny worm, bereft of his parents' love.

At then end of the handwork hour, the girls had knitted knee warmers and head protectors to be included in Christmas packages. In her kindly manner, Fräulein Hering asked what the students would like to knit next. Some of them shouted, "baby jackets, baby shirts, baby clothes."

The teacher was very surprised. Up to that point, the class had only been working for the soldiers.

"What will our boys in field gray do with baby clothes?" she laughed.

"Nothing. The clothes will be for Annemarie Braun's East Prussian child," said Hilde Rabe, the most outspoken member of the class.

Fräulein Hering asked for Annemarie's account. Nesthäkchen told in her rambling way the story of the living doll, and said that the infant, who had made too much racket for Grandmother, had migrated to the apartment of the porter's wife. "But I visit him every day to see how things are going. The porter's wife is very good to him."

A chorus of patriotic voices rang out. "Five pennies in the foreign word box. We say *housemaster*, not *porter*."

Blushing, Annemarie Braun fished five pennies from her pocket. Marlene Ulrich tossed them into the box, which had been Annemarie's purview.

Fräulein Hering's sympathy had been aroused. "It's good of you to want to sew for the foundling. But baby shirts and baby jackets aren't enough. The baby will need many other things. I suggest that the sixth class take responsibility for the child's education, should the parents not be found. I will personally direct your efforts. Are you able to bring twenty-five pennies for the foundling each month?"

"Of course! We can take that out of our pocket change," said the enthusiastic girls to one another.

"That will amount to a substantial sum to help defray the child's educational expenses. There are, alas, countless other children that the war has made into orphans. I will solicit contributions in the other classes. Each class shall assume responsibility for the welfare of one orphan," said the philanthropic teacher.

"We want Annemarie's child. We want to keep Hindenburg," pleaded the children.

"Whom do you want?" asked Fräulein Hering, thinking she hadn't understood.

"Annemarie named him Hindenburg—-"

The teacher laughed heartily.

"How did you arrive at this name, Annemarie?"

"It is the most beautiful name of all," answered the eager girl. "But now he's called Max or, more often, Mäxchen."

The whole class laughed.

"What will we name our new society? It must have a name," Fräulein Hering asked her students.

There were many suggestions: "East Prussian Society—Babe-in-Arms Society—German Girl Helpers—German Educational Society."

Fräulein Hering thought that none of these names was quite right.

"We want to call ourselves *Young Girls' Helpers Society*, the teacher suggested. This was the name that stuck.

The *Young Girls' Helpers Society* accepted its duties with colossal seriousness. Some of the girls asked their mothers for young children's clothes they had kept. Because most of the students no longer had little sisters, the society collected a substantial quantity of shirts, jackets, caps, diapers, and moccasins. The little East Prussian refugee Mäxchen soon had a wardrobe fit for a prince.

Fräulein Hering, the logical director of the *Young Girls' Helpers Society*, raised some objections. First, the students had the duty to dress the foundling simply and modestly. Second, there were many children who were equally needy. And third, the students should personally help the baby with their diligent efforts. This was better for the girls' own souls than to simply hand in clothing they had been given.

So in the end, tiny Max got only part of the clothing. The remainder went to foundling homes, care centers for small children, and above all, the East Prussian Committee, which was always overwhelmed with suffering to relieve.

The *Young Girls' Helpers Society* had one handwork hour weekly. The second hour was, as always, for the making of gifts of love for the brave soldiers, who should by no means receive short shrift.

Doctor's Nesthäkchen was too clumsy to knit clothing. The tomboy had a much more difficult time than the feminine Margot, who finished each article perfectly. Annemarie made touching efforts to do as well as her friend.

Not out of envy. No, it was for "our warriors."

Nesthäkchen's enthusiasm was not the cause of her abject failure to produce adequate woolens; rather, she was always in a hurry. The first pair of woolen gloves she finished had nine fingers. She forgot the tenth.

Annemarie was nonetheless able to console herself. "Certainly there are soldiers who have had one finger shot off. They need gloves, too. All of you are working for men who are the healthiest." Thus she was able comfort herself and deflect the teasing of her friends.

The boot inserts the children made of newspaper, for the winter campaign against Russia, were quite effective foot warmers. But for Annemarie Braun they were impossible. Even Fräulein Hering, for whom Annemarie was teacher's pet, could not restrain herself. "The poor soldier who must walk around on your inserts, Annemarie. He'll have bunions after his first march."

Annemarie laughed along with the class at the results of the competition, which did not offend her in the least. She crocheted her knee-warmers together above and below, so they would be very warm. But even if the German soldier everywhere stormed forward and was unafraid of any obstacle, he would still find it difficult to fight his way into Annemarie's knee-warmers. To open them top and bottom would improve them. Nesthäkchen made this alteration most unwillingly.

She did receive a field postcard with a funny poem from Uncle Heinrich, to whom she had sent a head protector. Uncle Heinrich thanked his niece fervently for leaving enough room in the head protector so that he wasn't choked, even though one side did press on his brain. Annemarie happily read the end of the poem in class:

> It protects against head knocking
> But I'll wear it as a stocking.

After Nesthäkchen had bestowed a truss on her father, he wrote back asking whether she thought he was a hippopotamus. The truss was of such enormous dimensions that the entire military hospital could fit into it.

Father's letter was not a happy one. Despite the hard work and all the tragedy he had witnessed, he himself was fine. But he was horribly worried about his wife, about whom no one had heard a word.

Every morning after she sprang out of bed, Annemarie ran, most often barefoot in her nightgown, to the front door, as soon as she heard the package of letters fall through the mail slot. Always in vain. There was never a letter from Mommy, or a reply to Grandmother's letter sent through Holland.

Nesthäkchen wrote to her daddy a proud account of her experiences as mother to a babe-in-arms, to try to cheer him up. She told him about the Young Girls' Helpers Society which had been organized in her school, and which was now mothering East Prussian refugee children.

Annemarie was overjoyed when her caring father sent her a contribution of 20 marks for the Society treasury. As a former foster mother, she had been named to the honorable job of overseeing the educational fund, and she collected contributions on the first of the month. The worst part of the job was the bookkeeping, since she had to carefully record every donation. Without Fräulein's help, she would have botched this work, as she was always in a hurry.

The baby carriage with the lustily thrashing Mäxchen stood on the street in the warm October sun, as Annemarie and Margot were on their way to school. Of course, they had to stop and look.

"Margot, he definitely laughed at me. He already knows me," said Annemarie overjoyed.

Margot, painfully punctual, would linger no longer. She ran off to avoid being late for class.

Annemarie could not pull herself away from her infant ward so easily. When she finally left him, despite her long strides, she was unable to overtake Margot.

Heavens, the clock was striking three; afternoon instruction had begun. Fräulein Drehmann would be rightly angry. Nesthäkchen's excuse—that she was late because of a foster child of the Young Girls' Helpers Society—would be unacceptable. She would get a black mark in her record.

Annemarie began to run. Without looking right or left, she dashed into the red schoolhouse, climbed the steps, and opened the door to the sixth class.

Appalled, she drew back. Instead of the girlish heads bent over their notebooks, Annemarie saw laughing soldiers. Everywhere, on benches and tables, men in field gray polished their boots, burnished their swords, and sang patriotic songs.

When they saw the surprised blond girl, the soldiers fell silent. "So, little girl, do you want to help us?" they said mirthfully.

Annemarie raised her hand to her forehead. Had she ended up in the wrong place? Was she in the barracks that was near the Volksschule? No, there on the wall was the map of Africa, which she had used yesterday.

"Where have all the girl students gone? Why are soldiers here?" Doctor's otherwise so clever Nesthäkchen did not know what was wrong.

"We are your new teachers. We are supposed to give the girls gymnastics instruction," said one joker. The other soldiers laughed. Finally a kindly old home guardsman, who himself had children at home, took pity on the puzzled girl.

"Oh, little mouse, don't let them fool you. The school has been turned into a barracks from top to bottom, because we don't have enough housing. We will be working diligently here, instead of you…"

"Yes, but where are all my classmates?" asked Annemarie, on the verge of tears.

The men shrugged their shoulders. "Probably they went home. You children are already smart enough. During war you don't have to learn anything." The soldiers' jibes were continual.

The usually happy Annemarie was not enjoying herself today. She felt badly that she had lingered when she should have rushed. But if the other children had been sent home, she would have been, too; certainly Margot, who had the same route to school. The tears, which the girl had restrained with difficulty, began to flow freely. She had to press her handkerchief into service. Where should she go now?

Figure 5. Instead of the girlish heads bent over their notebooks, Annemarie saw laughing soldiers.

Soldiers were everywhere. Their songs resounded from every classroom and every corridor. Downstairs in the courtyard, where the children had gone during recess, the soldiers washed their drill jackets in the fountain. Hesitantly, Annemarie stood at the entrance. Should she simply cut classes and go home? No. The high-spirited girl was a diligent student who could not break old habits.

Slowly she strolled to the corner, where here brother's high school was located. Classes there were long over.

Hello, what was this? From the schoolyard came voices, which hummed and droned like those she heard during class breaks. But this was Wednesday, when the boys didn't have afternoon instruction. The curious girl looked through the open front door at the schoolyard.

Say, weren't those blue, red, and white girls' dresses she saw through the crack in the doorway?

Excitedly, Annemarie drew nearer.

Suddenly someone was tugging on her blond locks.

"All right, who's hanging around outside, rather than in the courtyard, as school rules dictate?" It was cheerful old Professor Herwig, the acting principal.

His hardly melodic voice sounded to Annemarie like the song of an angel.

"Oh, professor, can you tell me where our school is. I can't find it. Soldiers are in all the classrooms," said Annemarie with a curtsey.

"Where is the school?" laughed the professor. "I call that not being able to see the forest for the trees. Can't you hear the noise of the break between classes?" The old gentleman gestured to the courtyard.

"We're here now?" Annemarie embraced the old professor, ecstatic to have arrived at her destination after a few wrong turns.

"We're being housed here for a few days, until we can find other shelter," joked Professor Herwig, who saw the gleam of happiness in Nesthäkchen's young blue eyes. "But tell me," he added more seriously, "why weren't you brought here with the other girls. Were you excused for an hour?"

If she said "yes," she could avoid unpleasant consequences. Nesthäkchen vacillated for a moment—only one.

"I came too late," she said softly. Annemarie was an honest child.

"So you see, your tardiness has itself punished you."

Nesthäkchen thought she had emerged from the situation unscathed, certainly without a lecture.

But her tardiness would continue to punish her.

"How amazed the boys will be that I am going to their high school," thought Annemarie proudly as she entered the schoolyard.

With a loud "Hello," her four friends greeted her. They laughed heartily when Nesthäkchen told them in her humorous way how she had visited the soldiers.

She learned from her friends that the students had not entered their class-rooms that day. They had assembled in the schoolyard and were directed from there to the high school. But the faithful Margot had been concerned about what had happened to her dilatory friend.

Annemarie told her companions how adorable Max was, and how happily he had giggled.

"He has every right to be cheerful, the brat. My brother Klaus says Max is already as rich as Croesus. Father sent us a twenty-mark bill for our Young Girls' Helpers Society. I brought it with me. I'm going to give ten marks to Fräulein Hering. Here's the money." Grandly Annemarie reached into her dress pocket, to display the treasure for her friends.

Suddenly she went pale. She withdrew her hand empty.

"My purse. My mussel-shaped purse from Wittdünn, where can it be?" Uncomprehendingly she again searched her pocket. "I certainly had it with me when I went to school. When I was running I felt it bumping my knee." She resumed the frantic search.

Her friends gathered around her, regarding her with startled eyes.

"Take another look in your pocket, Annemarie," said Ilse Hermann.

Nesthäkchen withdrew a crushed handkerchief, a top, two pieces of sugar, many pencil points, and a tiny rubber ball, but no mussel-shaped purse.

Doctor's Nesthäkchen began to howl vociferously. Curious girls from all the classes gathered around the sobbing child.

"When school is over, we'll go back to the *Volksschule*. Maybe you lost your purse on the way here," said the practical Marlene sympathetically.

The huge loss had left Margot without any words of consolation.

"I'm sure I lost my purse when I pulled out my handkerchief in the class-room," the poor thing clamored. "Oh, what will I do now? It wasn't my money. It belonged to the Young Girls' Helpers Society."

"If you didn't donate it and it came from your father, it still belongs to you," said Marianne.

Annemarie was frightfully anguished. "No, no, it doesn't belong to me. It belongs to Max, who has no parents or homeland. I've destroyed the worm's first fortune."

Amidst all the yammering, advising, and searching, the school bell rang, call-ing the students to class.

"Ask Fräulein Drehmann if you can go to look for your purse," suggested Marianne.

"We're writing our class essay. We've already wasted a lot of time moving from one building to another," said the conscientious Margot, who would not dream of missing the class essay.

Annemarie decided to ignore Marianne's suggestion, less from pangs of conscience than from reluctance to make Fräulein Drehmann aware that Annemarie had been tardy and missed the first hour of school.

Where had the proud feelings gone, which had possessed Annemarie when she entered her brother's school? With her head bowed she entered the room behind her friends.

As a result of the tumult associated with the move, Fräulein Drehmann didn't seem to have noticed Annemarie's absence during the first hour. She launched immediately into the class essay.

What sacrifices does the war demand from us, children? was the theme. In the first quarter hour Fräulein Drehmann discussed with the girls the content of the essay. She asked the students to list the sacrifices that they themselves had made in the first months of the war. They must write the sacrifices down in an attractive manner, filling not more than four pages.

Annemarie had just lost twenty marks she was supposed to contribute today. Could anyone believe that, anguished as she was, she could collect her thoughts sufficiently to compose a single sentence? She hid her face behind the blond head of Ilse, who sat in front of her, and stained her notebook with tears instead of ink.

"You must start writing," Margot whispered to her. From the other side, Marlene prodded Annemarie with her elbow.

Fräulein Drehmann noticed.

"Yes? What are you three in the corner up to? Everyone must do her own writing. Oh, Annemarie, are you crying? Can't you write your essay? You have already written so many good ones."

The teacher walked to the first bench. Astonished, she saw that Annemarie's page was blank.

"What does this mean, Annemarie? Why aren't you participating?"

Annemarie didn't want to answer. Her tears were choking her.

Marlene Ulrich volunteered the story.

"That's a result of children carrying too much money. You don't bring twenty marks to school," said Fräulein Drehmann with annoyance.

"I wanted to bring the money for the Young Girls' Helpers Society. Father had donated it to the society," said Annemarie in a pained, hesitant way.

"Tears won't make things better, Annemarie. Quite the opposite, you won't be able to do your assignment. Now collect your thoughts and start writing," said Fräulein Drehmann.

Oh, that was easier said than done. Annemarie tried and tried to write something. She had a lively creativity, a fresh style, and her writing had become quite good as a result of all the letters she had sent home from the children's sanatorium.

Today nothing came. Annemarie struggled. The war had demanded more sacrifices from her than from the other girls, even though everyone had a father or big brother at the front.

Indeed, Annemarie was separated from both parents, and her mommy was far away. Thoughts of mommy drove thoughts about the lost purse from Nesthäkchen's mind. Suddenly, her pen began to fly over the paper. All her soulful longing for Mother, her greatest war sacrifice to date, Annemarie transformed into written words.

Amazed, Margot regarded the torrent of words flowing from Annemarie's pen. Margot herself had to go over a sentence ten times in her mind, and usually scratched it out at least once after she had written it.

All of Annemarie's words were not drenched in tears. She smiled when she described the sleep she had lost on account of the screaming East Prussian infant. Her sleepless night was another war sacrifice. From tiny Max a small step led to the lost twenty marks, the final war sacrifice at the end of her essay. She had finished writing before most of her classmates.

"Bravo, Annemarie," said Fräulein Drehmann. "You strove to dutifully direct your thoughts. Now I'm going to excuse you to go to our former school and search for your lost purse."

Annemarie curtseyed gratefully, put on her sailor cap, and hurried off to begin her second search amidst the soldiers.

Most of the men were exercising in the courtyard. They stared curiously at the little interloper, now red in the face.

A sergeant asked her directly what she was looking for.

"My purse, my small mussel-shaped purse with twenty marks inside." Annemarie spoke anxiously, though she was not easily frightened.

The sergeant became friendlier. "Men, did one of you find a purse with twenty marks?"

None of the soldiers uttered a word. But the old home guardsman, who had been so friendly to her, stepped forward.

"I report most obediently that the little girl took out her handkerchief in the classroom where we were billeted. Perhaps the purse fell out of her pocket at that time.

"Go with her, Müller, and have a look," commanded the sergeant.

Annemarie took a deep breath. She made her most respectful curtsey to the sergeant and followed the kindly home guardsman into the building.

The tables and benches had already been removed. Bed frames replaced them. Annemarie and the home guardsman looked everywhere, in vain.

With a heavy heart, Nesthäkchen decided to head home. On the way, she determined to ask Grandmother to replace the lost twenty marks with money from the elderly lady's own savings account. This request would salve Annemarie's conscience.

When Annemarie got home, the ardently sought purse from Wittdünn with the twenty marks lay on the nursery table. The forgetful girl had not put it in her pocket when she left the house.

CHAPTER 10

▼

VERA

It rained from morning to night, all day long, unceasingly, genuine November rain. The rain washed the streets of Berlin clean. The people hastened to shelter. But the gray skies did not dampen the joy of victory in the people. No one thought of herself when she came home soaked, only of those outside.

"Our poor soldiers in their trenches," almost everyone sighed, when bad weather threatened. And in the evening, when a city dweller lay in her warm bed as the rain pounded the window panes, she didn't congratulate herself on her happy circumstances, for she knew that her bold defenders lay in wet earthen ditches.[1]

---

1. Else Ury makes no mention of the disaster for Germany that had occurred before this chapter begins. German military planning predicted that the French commander, Joseph Joffre, would move his troops east in the event of war. Joffre obliged. The Germans blocked the French offensives with horrifying casualties. 27,000 French soldiers died on August 22, 1914. But because of indecisiveness of Helmuth von Moltke, the German commander, Joffre was able to pull his army back toward Paris in time to meet the main German force on the Marne and defeat it in September. The Germans had lost forever the chance to smash France with a single crushing blow. The bloody trench warfare, which Else Ury mentions but does not account for, had begun.

Even Nesthäkchen felt remorse, when at night she rested quietly in her pretty nursery. She thought not only of her father and Uncle Heinrich, but of the many thousands outside who gladly accepted all privations.

During the gray rainy days, Nesthäkchen, with her cheerful disposition, was once again the sunshine in the house. How Grandma needed her. Why had her daughter Elsbeth, Nesthäkchen's mother, not written? Letters were coming from England. Grandmother knew many families who had received them. Why hadn't the elderly lady gotten one?

In the first days of the war, the English allowed German women to leave the country. Why had Elsbeth remained in England, when during these difficult times she should have been compelled to return home? Grandmother broke her old white-haired head on this conundrum, and the young children broke theirs, too.

Annemarie had much else to think about. Her school had been relocated once more, this time to the north of the city. This change was highly disagreeable for most of the students, as well as for the teachers who lived in western Berlin. But for the fatherland everyone gladly got up one hour earlier. The time was needed to traverse the longer path to school.

It was still dark when the two friends, Margot and Annemarie, set off for school in the morning. Here and there in the rainy gloom, gas lanterns on the street were still burning. Actually, the girls could have left home half an hour later, since they received twenty pennies daily for the electrified tram. But the two preferred to walk in the rain and donate their tram fare to the military hospital Christmas fund.

Of course, Fräulein noticed that Annemarie left home early and returned late with her loden coat dripping wet. The child could have stayed dry by taking the tram. It was not difficult for Fräulein to discover the cause of Annemarie's drenchings. The honest Nesthäkchen immediately revealed where her tram fare was going.

"Dear Fräulein, you won't prevent me from contributing, will you? Our warriors must endure for us more than this little bit of rain."

Fräulein objected. "You will catch your death of cold, Annemiechen, if you sit in school the entire afternoon in wet socks and damp clothes. It's quite enough if you save your groschen for the wounded during dry weather." This was what happened, despite Nesthäkchen's pleas. Margot's mother also forbade her daughter's wet wanderings. Consequently, the two friends still went to school together.

Much in the school had changed, besides the buildings and the location. All of the young male teachers had been inducted into the army. Female teachers replaced them. Two teachers had already been killed, and the girls mourned for them. But nobody had a spotless conscience. There were still girlish high jinks and girls who didn't please their teachers. How gladly the miscreants would have atoned after it was too late.

The circle of schoolgirls had changed. East Prussian children, forced with their parents from their homeland, were enrolled, many for months, others for weeks. Many German families were forced out of German Russia and Poland, while many others had fled. They sent their children to school in Berlin.

In the sixth class, a girl from Czernowitz had enrolled.[2] Her name was Vera Burkhard. Although her father was German, Vera spoke only Polish. She was a gorgeous child, with long black locks, a sensitive face, and anxious blue eyes. The poor thing was completely lost among all the German children.

She knew only a few words of German. She was unable to grasp what the teachers were saying in class. While they lectured, she sat bored, not taking notes. On her blotting paper she drew dolls and animals. The teachers were unable to rebuke her because she didn't understand them.

The worst time for Vera was the recess between classes. The other girls giggled and laughed together. They embraced passionately, gathered together in the schoolyard in happy groups, and walked about with one another. Meanwhile, Vera, in a corner by herself, regarded them with longing eyes. Nobody came up to her or invited her to take part in the cheerful activity.

Why was Vera so isolated? Why did the other girls keep away from her? She was a warm, sympathetic person. And the Cossacks had forced her to flee her homeland, just like all the other refugee children.

Vera's problems began the first day of school. Margot and Annemarie sympathized with the petite foreign girl and asked her to join them during recess. They communicated their request simply. Annemarie took Vera by one arm, Margot by the other. All three laughed. Everything went fine. Margot indicated that she liked Vera's green plaid dress. Annemarie took half the chocolate bar Grandmother had put in her breakfast box and popped it into Vera's mouth.

Margot and Annemarie began speaking German, and Vera responded in Polish. Naturally, Annemarie and Margot could not understand her. But the linguis-

---

2. Czernowitz (now Chernovtsy, Ukraine) was part of Austria-Hungary in 1914, and lay 1200 km east of Berlin. It was a major focus of trade, an industrial center, and an important railway junction. In 1910, 48% of the people spoke German, while 17% spoke Polish. There was also a large population of Yiddish-speaking Jews.

tic difference was not crucial. Indeed, the girls laughed wildly about the hodgepodge of incomprehensible words.

But the verbal mishmash annoyed two bigger girls from the first class. "Ugh, look at those two walking arm in arm with our enemy," they said loudly, when they recognized that Vera was speaking Polish.

Horrified, Annemarie dropped Vera's arm. Was this Polish girl truly one of Germany's enemies? The interior of Annemarie's head was no more orderly than her shoe chest. She easily confused a Pole with a Russian.

Her confusion brought shame. How could she have dishonored Germany by walking arm-in-arm with the Polish-speaking Vera? How could a German girl be so unpatriotic? But the recess was over before Vera could sense that her new friends felt differently about her.

Annemarie became red all over as she whispered to Margot that she would have nothing more to do with Vera Burkhard. If she did, she would be a traitor to the fatherland.

"She's Polish, not Russian," said Margot.

"That doesn't make any difference. Does she speak German? No! Anybody who doesn't speak German is one of our enemies," said Annemarie ignorantly.

Good student that she was, Margot knew that Poland and Russia were not the same country. But she was a mild person, subservient to her lively friend. And Vera truly spoke hardly any German.

During the next class, the girls passed a note from one to another under the table: "Whoever associates with Vera Burkhard during recess or speaks to her betrays the fatherland." Vera did not see the note.

Nobody wanted to betray the fatherland. Every child wanted to be the most patriotic in the class.

The other girls felt attracted to the pretty, alien Vera. Anything novel is attractive to children. But they kept away from her nonetheless. The minatory note came from Annemarie Braun, the dominant girl, who was student liaison and treasurer of the Young Girls' Helpers Society. Anyone who ignored Annemarie's note risked becoming class pariah, a double-crosser of the fatherland. Suddenly Vera was an outcast.

Doctor's Nesthäkchen had no idea what an injustice she had perpetrated. Quite the contrary, Annemarie was quite proud to have rescued the class from a traitor.

During the next recess, after the evil note had made its rounds, Vera amicably approached Margot and Annemarie. Her bright blue eyes gleaming, she wanted to walk arm-in-arm again with her new friends.

Margot, blushing in her shy way, ignored Vera. The mercurial Annemarie, eyes blazing, yelled so loudly that everyone in the class could hear: "We want nothing to do with you, you old enemy!" Simultaneously, Annemarie yanked Margot away from Vera.

Vera hadn't understood a word. But she knew that the blond girl, from the sound of her voice, was not behaving in a friendly way.

Anyone would have been hurt by Annemarie's callous rejection, even if she didn't know German. And the contemptuous behavior of the other girls showed they had understood Annemarie's demand that they must defend themselves against all enemies.

During recess Vera was totally isolated. The otherwise sociable girls completely excluded her.

Vera racked her brains, trying to understand what she had done to alienate the attractive Annemarie, whom, among all the other girls, she liked best. Why had Nesthäkchen suddenly become so hostile toward her? Maybe she had misunderstood something, since her German was so poor. In any case, Vera would try to regain Annemarie's affection.

One day, Vera's aunt, with whom she was living, gave her an especially luscious apple to take to school. With a heavy heart, Vera decided to give the apple to Annemarie. No doubt this gift would win back Nesthäkchen's camaraderie.

Annemarie walked past Vera, staring intently through a hole she was boring in the air in order not to see her.

"There, please, take it," said Vera, using the few words of German she knew, as she held the splendid red apple to Annemarie's mouth.

Annemarie pushed away the proffering hand so violently that the apple flew out and rolled under the classroom cupboard.

"I won't take gifts from you," shouted Annemarie angrily.

Tears streamed from Vera's eyes as she bent down to retrieve her apple. The magnificent piece of fruit tasted terrible to her now.

"I won't go to school any more," said the sobbing Vera to her aunt after Nesthäkchen's crass rejection. Vera was supposed to speak German, but lapsed into Polish when she was upset. Her father had traveled frequently, and the servants spoke only Polish.

Vera's aunt, her father's sister, understood Polish. Before her marriage, she had spent considerable time in the house of her brother in Czernowitz, because Vera's mother, who was Polish, had died young.

"Darling, why don't you want to go back to school?" asked Vera's astonished aunt.

"The children are so hateful to me. None of them want anything to do with me. I want to go back to my girlfriends in Czernowitz," cried the child piteously.

"Speak German, Vera," admonished her aunt. "If you always speak Polish, the children in school won't understand you. No wonder they don't want anything to do with you. The faster you learn German, the faster they will befriend you."

But was poor German Vera's only problem? Annemarie and Margot had embraced Vera during the first recess, and Vera hadn't spoken a single German word.

Vera's father, who was fighting as a volunteer against the Russians at Augustow, answered his daughter's plaintive letter with the identical solution Vera's aunt had suggested. Vera needed to learn German as soon as possible, he wrote, in order to mix with the other children. Now Vera began in earnest to make the difficult German language her own.

"Aren't we unjust to treat Vera Burkhard so horribly?" said Ilse Hermann to Marlene Ulrich one day. "It's not her fault that her mother was Polish. And her father is certainly German."

Marlene had been thinking the same thing. "Maybe we should accept her."

"No, then Annemarie would be through with us, and all the other children would think we were unpatriotic." False shame smothered the good impulses in the hearts of the two girls.

Annemarie was Vera's worst enemy and called her the *Polack*. The naughty Annemarie was convinced that she had to set a "good example" as to how Vera should be treated.

One day, the rain fell in torrents. Annemarie had no umbrella. Indeed, every day she forgot something. One day it was her box of pens, one day her notebook, one day her breakfast or her rubbers. Today it was the umbrella. She had looked out the window early in the morning and seen the rain, but was careless nevertheless.

Annemarie walked to school with Margot Thielen, who never forgot her umbrella or anything else. Margot took Annemarie gladly under the umbrella, which was very pleasant for both of them.

Margot had to meet her mother after school. Mrs. Thielen planned to take Margot to buy a winter coat.

"Don't worry," said Annemarie, "the rain will have stopped long before school is over.

But at noon it was still raining "little cobbler boys," as the Berliners like to say.

To Doctor's Nesthäkchen, who had already had one shower, the weather was crazy. The rain was falling in such torrents that the balconies of buildings, which ordinarily served as tram stop shelters, were of no use at all.

Annemarie heard rushing footsteps behind her. It sounded as if someone was coming to pick her up. She turned her head and saw another schoolgirl, her face hidden behind an umbrella. Annemarie did not move and allowed the other girl to approach her. Maybe the stranger was from her class and wanted to take Annemarie to the tram stop under the umbrella.

The hurrying umbrella drew nearer. A delicate, blushing, pretty face, framed by black locks, was visible under a brown leather sou'wester. It was the *Polack*.

Annemarie turned her back straightaway and hastened off through the pounding rain. Why did Vera want to run after her?

Despite Annemarie's quick pace, Vera stayed hard on her heels. Overtaking the dripping blond girl, Vera raced alongside her.

"Come, please, under my umbrella." In a short time, diligent Vera had made remarkable progress in German. But she still had not mastered the guttural German *r*, which sounds like a snore coming deep from the throat. The other students often laughed at her efforts. But Annemarie did not laugh as Vera held out the umbrella.

What impudence, thought Annemarie, her eyes blazing with indignity. "I'm not going anywhere with you under your umbrella, *Polack*."

Despite her strides in German comprehension, Vera did not know what *Polack* meant. She knew only that Annemarie Braun didn't want any part of her or her umbrella.

"Take the umbrella. I have a rubber raincoat. I won't get very wet," said Vera, offering the umbrella to her enemy.

The blood shot into Nesthäkchen's face. But she was not indignant; she was painfully ashamed. For the first time, she realized how wickedly she had treated the *Polack*. Yet here was Vera offering Annemarie her own umbrella, and allowing herself to get soaked to the skin.

Annemarie wordlessly shook her head and ran to the tram stop.

Vera followed her slowly with a heavy heart.

By the time the electric tram pulled up, both girls were waiting at the stop. Vera lived in Charlottenburg and took the long tram ride every day.

Annemarie and Margot arranged their schedules so that they were never on the same tram with the *Polack*. But today Vera boarded the tram just behind Annemarie.

Figure 6. What impudence, thought Annemarie, her eyes blazing with indignity. "I'm not going anywhere with you under your umbrella, Polack."

Annemarie contorted her face angrily and bitterly. But her expression was not directed toward Vera. Rather, Nesthäkchen believed that her enemy, against whom she had turned the entire class, was a thousand times better person than she was herself.

The tram was packed.

"Go to the back door, children," said the lady conductor. Transit jobs formerly held by men now at the front had been taken over by women.

The two enemies were now squeezed together in the overfilled tram. With every jolt and bump of the car the girls fell into one another, both unwillingly.

Annemarie had paid her fare. Vera pulled out her purse. "I—I have only five pennies," she stuttered, anxiously fishing around in the purse. Would she be forced to get out?

"Your little school friend can pay the rest of the fare," said the conductor.

Vera looked at Annemarie with her gorgeous pleading eyes.

The little "friend" seemed oblivious to the entire situation. With studied indifference she gazed through the rain spattered windows at the gray downpour outside.

Yet her face revealed the pitched battle that was going on behind it. Annemarie had enough money with her. Shouldn't she give Vera the five pennies she needed, after Vera had volunteered her umbrella? Did she really want to see Vera forced out of the tram in this horrid weather?

But should a German girl help a *Polack?* No, never. Spurious love for the fatherland had again cowed Annemarie's heartfelt good impulses, which had almost triumphed.

"Here is the money for the little girl," said a friendly lady.

"Thank you very much," whispered Vera with trembling lips and a large tear glistening on her long eyelashes.

The tram made an abrupt turn, jarring the passengers and throwing Annemarie into Vera. Helplessly, Annemarie grasped Vera's arm with both hands to prevent herself from falling.

The blond child didn't even say "excuse me." She hastened from the tram, although it had not arrived at her station. Annemarie preferred a soaking to standing next to her enemy for another moment.

Annemarie did not feel hearty self-satisfaction. She was silent and oppressed. Her hateful conduct toward Vera had not brought her joy. Had she done the right thing? For the first time she had doubts.

Should she seek Grandmother's counsel? Oh, Grandmother's good heart would never countenance such deplorable behavior toward another child. Grandmother's clear, kindly eyes would surely shame her.

And Fräulein? She would doubtless denounce Annemarie's conduct. The girl was certain.

If only mommy were here. Mommy would understand her daughter and help her. Nesthäkchen's longing for her far-away mother had never been more ardent than it was today.

Hans was away on Pathfinder duty. But Klaus was in the room sticking little flags into the large war map. He followed every event at the front with a fascination he had never shown for his schoolbooks.

Kläuschen," said Annemarie, laying her hand on her brother's shoulder, "I have something to discuss with you."

Klaus did not want to be disturbed as he punctured Ypres with a black, white, and red flag.[3]

"Did you gobble up something that didn't agree with you?" said Klaus without interest.

"No, I mean, I don't know."

Klaus looked at his sister with contempt. He always knew when he had eaten something he shouldn't have.

"Did I tell you about the *Polack* in my school?" she asked.

---

3. With the failure of the German offensive against France at the Battle of the
   Marne, and the allied counter-offensive, the so-called 'race to the sea' began,
   a movement towards the North Sea coast as each army attempted to
   out-flank the other by moving progressively north and west. As they went,
   each army constructed a series of trench lines, starting on 15 September, that
   came to characterize war on the Western Front until 1918. Stalemate had set
   in. The First Battle of Ypres, a Belgian coastal town, began on 14 October
   when Erich von Falkenhayn, the German Chief of Staff, sent his Fourth and
   Sixth armies into Ypres. The battle started with a nine-day German offensive
   that was only halted with the arrival of French reinforcements and the
   deliberate flooding of the Belgian front. Belgian troops opened the sluice
   gates of the dikes holding back the sea from the low countries. The flood
   encompassed the final ten miles of trenches in the far north, and later proved
   a hindrance to the movement of allied troops and equipment. By December
   1914, the loss of life at Ypres had been horrendous on both sides. British
   casualties were reported at 58,155, mostly pre-war professional soldiers, a
   loss the British could ill-afford. French casualties were set at around 50,000,
   and German losses at 130,000 men.

"Yes, certainly. Did you have a tiff with her?"

"No but we have so much in common. Today she offered me her umbrella, and I was unwilling to lay out the five pennies she needed for the tram," said Annemarie, blushing at the memory.

"You did right. Our enemies have a lot in common, so we have to fight them all." Obviously Nesthäkchen had found a poor advisor.

"Above all, Annemie, the girl is nothing but a Russian spy." At the moment, Klaus thought of nothing but spies. Every foreign-looking person was a spy to him. Recently Klaus had stared too long at a policeman speaking English with a man who had an American accent, and the cop had slapped Klaus' face, saying "So my boy, from now on don't suspect everyone you see of being a spy."

The slap didn't cure Klaus of his spy mania for long. At the moment he was certain that Annemarie's *Polack* was a spy.

Could Klaus be correct? If so, Nesthäkchen had not rejected Vera strongly enough. Spies are people without honor, who betray their country for money, as Hans had recently explained to her.

Was Vera such a person? No, that was not possible, thought Annemarie; in her mind's eye, an image of the charming girl appeared.

Yet wasn't there a sign in all trains: "Soldiers, be careful when you talk. Danger—spies are everywhere"? If spies are everywhere, some must be in Berlin. Why shouldn't the Polish-speaking Vera be one of them? This thought soothed Annemarie. For a moment, the pangs of conscience she had suffered all day, a result of her hateful treatment of Vera, disappeared.

Next day in the sixth class, another note circulated under the table during a history lecture: "Be careful what you say. Danger—spies are everywhere."

Everyone in class knew to whom the note referred.

CHAPTER 11

▼

CHRISTMAS EVE IN THE MILITARY HOSPITAL

All of the students now avoided Vera more assiduously than ever before. Even the two girls, Ilse and Marlene, who had friendly feelings toward her, were forced to conform. A spy—ugh!

Things went so far that children conversing with one another dropped their voices when Vera was nearby, since most of them were talking about the war, and what they had learned in letters from relatives at the front. Now they whispered to one another and cast apprehensive glances at the *Polack*. Was she trying to hear what they were saying?

The men and women teachers were friendly and warm to the homeless foreigner, who was so diligent in her schoolwork. Yet instead of following their teachers' example, the children wondered whether they shouldn't tell the teachers that Vera was a Russian spy. But no one dared to, even the cheeky Annemarie Braun.

For a long time, Vera had caused her no remorse. Quite the contrary, whenever she could she showed "the spy" her contempt. On December 1, when she went from one girl to another to collect monthly contributions for the Young Girls' Helpers Society, Vera held out twenty-five pennies in her hand. Annemarie walked right by, as though she had not even noticed Vera's gesture.

During the next recess, the dark-haired girl walked over to Annemarie's desk. "I not yet paid," said Vera softly, putting the money into Annemarie's hand.

Annemarie allowed the coins to fall, as though they were glowing iron. "I won't take anything from you. You don't belong to our Young Girls' Helpers Society. Only German girls can be members," she said, looking proudly at her classmates.

The girls laughed and nodded in approval. Annemarie had done right to show the spy what everyone thought of her.

Vera's eyes filled with tears as she turned away.

Was she no German girl? Because she was German, she had to flee the Cossack invasion of her homeland. Her father was fighting for Germany as a volunteer, like the fathers of the other students. To be sure, she spoke Polish almost exclusively when she enrolled, but she had heard no other language from the family servants in Czernowitz.

Vera reflected and brooded, but could not understand why she was the only girl who could not join the Young Girls' Helpers Society. Annemarie's intense contempt had gripped her heart, leaving her depressed and sad.

This was the month that ordinarily brought joy to a child's heart. But this year the beautiful month of Christmas had a more serious face. Every family had a beloved member who had been called to arms—on land, at sea, or high up in the air. And how cruelly war had robbed the people of their dear ones. The streets were filled with black-veiled women.

No wonder the children's joy was subdued, more this year than in any other. Neither Annemarie nor her friends had written Christmas cards. Indeed, they had relinquished Christmas gifts, requesting that the money be used for packages sent to the front or provision of Christmas cheer for the wounded.

The Schubert Girls' Lyceum had sent mountains of packages to the front soldiers. For months, industrious feminine hands had exerted themselves for the fatherland's defenders. The girls had made thick carpets out of newspaper, to be laid on the bottom of the trenches to soak up moisture. They had knitted warm, brightly colored "goldfinch blankets" from leftover wool, as well as stockings, shawls, head and chest protectors, wrist warmers and abdominal bandages in an unending stream. Every school in every German city had taken part. German women and girls everywhere labored loyally for the German soldiers.

The soldiers still suffered, on Poland's icy plains, in the snow-covered forests of the Ardennes, in the glacial Carpathian Mountains, on the stormy Flemish coasts, and on the open sea. Doctor's Nesthäkchen sent her Christmas packages primarily to the navy. From her stay on the Baltic, she knew what a nocturnal winter storm on the high seas was like. Every packet, bound with a black, white, and red ribbon, held chocolate, tobacco, and cigarettes. Stockings were filled with apples, nuts, and gingerbread. Most important to the children, however, was the greeting card with each child's address. The card identified to the soldier, who wore the stockings or head protector, the name of the person who had labored for many weeks to make the article of clothing. The thank-you cards from happy soldiers were a rich reward.

A huge packet was sent to Dr. Braun, although the entire Braun household hoped that he might be home on leave for Christmas.

Annemarie had an additional desire, and persuaded herself that Mommy would also come home for the holidays. How could she be away from her children on Christmas Eve? To be sure, Annemarie had been far from home in the children's sanatorium, away from her parents, last Christmas. Somehow that didn't seem so bad. But this year? No, no, mommy must be here.

Grandmother had more modest wishes. She would be happy if only she had some word of her daughter. Meanwhile, together with Fräulein, she worked to prepare a lovely Christmas Eve for her grandchildren.

Of course, all three children had said they didn't want Christmas gifts. But where was there a grandmother who could allow her grandchildren to pass Christmas Eve empty-handed?

Christmas Eve of the Great War year settled softly on the furiously battling world. Was the bloody fight going on even today? No, the front was quiet everywhere. Instead of flashing grenades, lighted trees glimmered in the snowy forests. In the winter night, pious songs from rough male throats supplanted the clatter of machine guns. In the trenches, German soldiers celebrated Christmas.[1]

In the military hospital, Dr. Braun looked at his gigantic package from home with wistful eyes. How lovingly packed it was, how everyone in his family had worked to please him. His Nesthäkchen, what hadn't she done for him? She had even knitted him a muff.

---

1. During the 'Christmas Truce' of 1914, soldiers on the Western Front laid down their arms on Christmas Day and met in No Man's Land between the French and German lines. They exchanged food and cigarettes, and played football. The cessation of violence was entirely unofficial and there had been no prior discussion: troops acted spontaneously from goodwill, not orders. The leaders on both sides, among them Winston Churchill, were horrified and demanded that there be no recurrence of such an event.

Doctor Braun smiled. His daughter had envisioned the field hospital to be a frozen place amidst the trenches. In fact, the rooms were comfortably heated. But the knitted objects would serve the wounded well after they had left.

How gladly Dr. Braun would have renounced all the gifts, if only he could hold Nesthäkchen on his knee. His gaze fell on the little black and white ribbon adorning his buttonhole. As a Christmas gift, he had been awarded the Iron Cross for his tireless work, which he performed day and night.[2] But where was the joy that this decoration should have brought? If only he could have shared the honor with his wife. In fact, he had no idea whether the news of his Iron Cross would reach her, or whether she had any news of him at all. Why neither she nor any of their English relatives had written was a mystery.

The doctor's mind called forth memories of past Christmas Eves. He saw the tree sparkling with lights in the living room. He heard the rejoicing of his children.

Suddenly there was an ear-splitting crash, as a windowpane shattered. The instrument cabinet shook. Pale-faced nurses and ambulance attendants tumbled into the room. "Doctor, a French flying bomb—it fell on our hospital. Luckily it didn't explode."

"Hooligans—even the Red Cross on Christmas Eve is not sacred to them," said Dr. Braun indignantly, as he hurried off to tend to the wounded.

While the doctor in the far-off military hospital in France thought of home, Nesthäkchen was thinking of him. Her father had not gotten leave, to her boundless disappointment. But if she was true to herself, she would have been even more unhappy, because the hands of the white nursery clock went round and round, without any sign of Mother.

It was already four o'clock. Nesthäkchen had to prepare for the presentation of gifts in the school turned military hospital. At four-thirty, the girls of the sixth class were supposed to assemble in front of the former Schubert Lyceum with their Christmas packages. Fräulein Hering was waiting for them.

Every class gave gifts to a different military hospital, and many also had gifts for war orphans. Every student was supposed to bring along gingerbread, an apple, and nuts. The children created magnificent colorful trays with these small contributions.

Annemarie's eyes wandered around her room once more. Since her stay in the children's sanatorium, she had become accustomed to never leaving her room

2. Note that this was an Iron Cross second class. A first class Iron Cross had a pin on the back, not a ribbon.

without checking to see if she had left something lying around. No, everything was in order. In the far corner she had stacked the Christmas gifts and placed the empty dollhouse over them. Nobody would find them there.

Annemarie reached for the multitude of packets and packages. How could she carry them all? Hanne was still busy, and Klaus, who could have helped her, had gone with his teacher to another military hospital gift ceremony. Fräulein and Grandmother were trimming the tree in the living room.

Nesthäkchen was a resourceful girl. From her brother's closet she took Hans' roomy knapsack. Everything would fit inside it.

My goodness, it was heavy. But didn't the soldiers carry heavier packs on their backs during their exhausting marches? Forward! Margot was certainly already waiting downstairs.

Annemarie's friend, standing next to a white children's wagon, was in front of the snow-covered fence that enclosed the flowerbeds in front of the building. Was Margot bringing along her little sister in the wagon?

Not at all. Annemarie had to laugh and Margot laughed along with her. The children's wagon was piled with gifts. "Are you going mountain climbing, Annemarie?" said Margot, pointing at the knapsack.

Both girls struggled with their loads. But what was the weight of the packages in comparison to the exalted feeling of bringing Christmas joy to the wounded?

The girls gathered in the former school courtyard. Many of the smaller girls had used their doll wagons to transport gifts. In spite of the thaw, Hilde Rabe had brought her sled.

"What? Is the Polack here too?" cried Annemarie so loudly that Vera, standing next to her own gift basket, jumped.

Does Christmas Eve make people better? After all, everyone should only express love for her fellow man. Does this holiday soften the hearts of young girls?

Alas, the answer is no. The students of the sixth class, who felt such compassion for the wounded, themselves had wounded poor Vera with their hostile words and angry stares. Doctor's Nesthäkchen was the worst offender.

"If Fräulein Hering knew what we know, she would certainly never take Vera into a military hospital. How easy it will be for her to spy there," whispered Annemarie to her confidantes.

Happily, there was no more time to abuse Vera Burkhard. The children were led into the fir-decorated former school auditorium, where a tall Christmas tree twinkled and sparkled. On a long table under the tree lay the gift packages for the soldiers.

The girls felt pain in their hearts when the wounded, in their blue and white striped gowns, hobbled into the room on walking sticks or crutches, on the arms of nurses, or on stretchers or gurneys. Illness and misery confronted blithe youth.

The excited Margot reached for Annemarie's arm. The two girls were overwhelmed by unspeakable pity for the severely maimed men, many of whom couldn't even see the Christmas lights. Annemarie's blue eyes filled with tears, and she felt deeply ashamed. Had self-pity not consumed her the whole day because she couldn't celebrate Christmas with her father and mother? How lucky she was compared to these injured soldiers around her, who were also far from their loved ones on Christmas Eve.

Despite the suffering they had to endure, the men's pale faces looked content and grateful. The German soldier shows his courage and sacrifice not only in battle, but also when confronting his relentless fate.

From the blazing Christmas tree, the wounded warriors gazed at the flocks of blossoming children surrounding them on all sides. The soldiers' faces lit up. It was as though their own blond daughter or little sister at home was waiting to present them with gifts.

One of the doctors sat down at the piano and played *Silent Night*. The music lent enchantment to the unusual Christmas festivities. Deep masculine voices mixed with young girlish ones. Tears appeared in the battle-hardened warriors' eyes, and no one was ashamed.

When the song ended, one of the nurses approached the girls. "So, children, now Santa Claus can pay a visit to our soldiers."

"Sister Elfriede," cried Nesthäkchen ecstatically. Before Margot noticed, Annemarie had hurried to the other side of the room, to a nurse with a kindly face and brown cap. "Sister Elfriede, don't you know me anymore? I'm Annemarie Braun. You nursed me back to health in my father's clinic when I had scarlet fever."[3]

"Girl, how big and strong you are. I would never have recognized you." Sister Elfriede happily squeezed the hand of her former patient.

All eyes were directed at the delightful blond girl and the joyful reunion.

The other children distributed their packages. Annemarie handed hers out with friendly words to each recipient. Soon, conversations had commenced

---

3. Scarlet fever, a dreaded infection of childhood, occurred in devastating epidemics with a 30% mortality rate. Since the introduction of antibiotics, scarlet fever has become uncommon and for unknown reasons less deadly.

between the girlish gift-givers and the recipients. The soldiers told where they had been wounded, and the children listened attentively.

Annemarie glanced worriedly at Vera. Would she pass on the information she got here?

Vera stood opposite Annemarie and a blinded soldier. The compassionate Vera felt drawn to the unlucky man, while the other children avoided any contact with him.

Vera proceeded to give the soldier a bag of gingerbread and marzipan. Annemarie hurried to intercede. Heavens, was the spy trying to poison German soldiers?

"You are a dear little girl," Annemarie heard the blind soldier say to Vera. He softly stroked Vera's lovely face, which he was unable to see. "Do you also have relatives at the front?"

"Yes, my papa," Vera replied softly.

"Either the Polack is lying, or her father is fighting against the Germans," thought Annemarie.

The soldier reached for a little bag that he had tied himself. "Here, little girl, I give this to you in memory of this Christmas Eve, which you have brightly illuminated for a blind man."

Vera blushed with joy. But Annemarie stared balefully at Vera, dissipating her joy. Was Nesthäkchen envious?

Not at all. She was furious that the Polack, surely a spy, should enjoy such recognition. If the German soldier only knew the truth.

Fräulein Hering promised to visit the military hospital again with her students. Annemarie said goodbye to Sister Elfriede. The soldiers waved thankful greetings to their little benefactors.

On the staircase, Vera tried to approach Annemarie.

"Do you want the bag? Please, take it," said Vera, shyly holding out the little sack that had been such a joy to her.

Annemarie was dismayed. She was a good child. Only false love for the fatherland had hardened her heart against Vera. But Vera's touching words had undermined the artificial wall of contempt for her that Annemarie had built.

"I thank you. You did deserve this gift," said Annemarie kindly.

Then Annemarie went home, arm in arm with Margot, Ilse, and Marlene. Vera followed by herself.

Vera was not sad. Indeed, she was happier than she had been in a long time. "Dear God, I thank you, because Annemarie was friendlier toward me than she has ever been," she thought happily.

Annemarie too had feelings of satisfaction. Did these feelings come from the joy the wounded men had given her, or from her better treatment of Vera? Annemarie had no answer.

Bells rang out in the brightly illuminated Kaiser Wilhelm Memorial Church. "Peace on earth," they chanted. But when would peace on earth arrive?

CHAPTER 12

▼

FINALLY A MESSAGE

The first day of Christmas blinked through the crack in the nursery window curtains. Nesthäkchen, in her white bed, blinked too. Annemarie had become so used to getting up early for school that even on holidays she was unable to oversleep.

It was quite agreeable to doze a little in bed and think of yesterday's Christmas Eve. The day went well enough, although her parents weren't present. Only when Fräulein called Annemarie to open her gifts, and Daddy and Mommy were not waiting at the Christmas tree, did tears well up in Nesthäkchen's eyes. But she gritted her teeth. No, Grandma would not allow her granddaughter to be sad. Good old Grandma! With what love she had listened to each grandchild to overhear his or her every wish.

Annemarie didn't want to appear ungrateful. She got the sweet little clock she had always wanted. Was it any wonder that her sadness vanished?

And what a wonderful Christmas Annemarie had planned. Grandmother would not miss mommy. To that end, Nesthäkchen herself had prepared the Christmas table, which Grandmother had always taken care of. The girl's efforts were noteworthy. She had provided a hook for the key ring, which was always disappearing. She got Grandma a pair of steel rimmed glasses to use when she mislaid her gold-rimmed ones.

"Look here, woolen ear muffs. Shall I send them to the front, darling?" asked Grandmother with a smile. Annemarie told her they were to protect her chapped ears, from which she had been suffering, and the elderly lady began to laugh.

Sweets, too, were part of a proper Christmas table. Annemarie had furnished a stick of licorice, as well as two pennies' worth of carob and taffy—the sweets that she liked to nibble on herself. No wonder that the grandchildren's happiness had banished Grandmother's ominous thoughts about her far off daughter.

To a pleased Aunt Albertinchen, Nesthäkchen gave a head protector that was too small for the soldiers, in case the lady should get a toothache. Rejoicing prevailed in the Braun household, despite the absence of father and mother.

But in the gray dawn, yesterday's happiness vanished. Why hadn't Annemarie received even a Christmas card from mommy? Didn't mommy think about her children any more?

Hanne's carpet cleaner rumbled in the next room. Fräulein didn't want to get up. The doorbell rang and a package of letters fell through the slot. Like a gust of wind Annemarie raced to the front door. She made this dash every day, and every day she was disappointed. Would today be different?

The newspaper, a field post card to Hans, but what was this? Nesthäkchen's eyes widened. Here was mommy's familiar handwriting, which the girl had not seen for many months.

"Grandma! Fräulein! A letter! A letter from mommy!" Annemarie yelled in the somnolent house as though the place were on fire.

People tumbled from every doorway in strange garments. But who noticed that Grandmother, in her excitement, was wearing her violet dressing gown inside out? Who looked at Fräulein, who had wrapped herself in a tablecloth instead of her warm robe? Or that Hans, in his haste, had pulled on Klaus' pants. All eyes were directed at the letter, written on thin paper, which Nesthäkchen was waving in the air like a victory banner.

The always anxious Grandmother had not noticed that Annemarie was running around in bare feet, and this oversight said much about the event.

The letter was addressed to Grandmother.

"My glasses, my God, where have I left my glasses?" said Grandmother, furiously searching. Annemarie quickly brought the steel-rimmed Christmas glasses—what a provident gift. But when Grandmother set the frames on her nose, there were no lenses.

"You have to let the optician put in the lenses, because I didn't know your correction," explained Annemarie.

Figure 7. "Grandma! Fräulein! A letter! A letter from mommy!" Annemarie yelled in the somnolent house as though the place were on fire.

Grandmother couldn't wait any longer. Hans offered to read the letter out loud. In the meantime, Fräulein covered cold, shivering Annemarie with a warm blanket.

"Dear Mother, my dear, dear children," Hans began. "I just got your letter by way of Holland. It must have been in the mail for weeks. I was dismayed to learn that you had never received my many letters, and you were terribly worried about me. I have been writing you at least twice a week, sometimes more often. As you may imagine, I am constantly thinking of you. I asked Cousin Charles Edward to find out why my letters did not reach you, since there is still mail service from here to Germany, but he was unable to determine. I do know that I wrote quite clearly about my feelings and wishes for our dearest fatherland, without realizing that the English censors would read every line. My cousin believes that the censors would not release my letters. There is no other explanation. This time, I will not express my feelings so that my letter will get through. I will limit myself to repeating the facts, of which I presume you have long been aware.

"The declaration of war surprised us. In our rural isolation we hardly read the newspaper. Cousin *Annchen* and I were doubly shocked. I was sick with anguish and naturally I wanted to come home immediately. I worried about all of you, especially my little *Lotte,* who was still alone in the Baltic, and my husband, who was to leave for the front. My cares undermined my health and I began running a high fever. I was delirious for days, and when I finally regained consciousness, German women were not permitted to leave England. You can imagine how unhappy I was to be away from you in these great times. Although my cousin is absolutely, unrepentantly against me, he is English and hopes that his people will be victorious, just as I hope for a German victory. But cousin Annchen was born in Germany and is still German in her heart. She is only English by marriage, and for her the situation is difficult. Opposed emotions pull the poor thing this way and that. You can't imagine how frightful I find it these days to be immobilized in the enemy's country, when the full strength of a German woman should be devoted to the welfare of her people. I look forward to the moment when Germans will again be allowed to leave England. May God allow this moment to come soon, because I am sick with longing for all of you and for the fatherland.

"I have had very little news of you, perhaps for the same reason that you didn't receive my letters, that is, the censors. Besides your last letter by way of Holland, I have gotten only postcards from the children. From these messages I at least know that they returned home safely and that you, dear Mother, have cared lovingly for my orphaned chicks. Sincere thanks for all your love. Our Fräulein's being there to assist you is a comfort to me. I hope that my little Lotte will help her beloved Grandmother as much as she can. I also hope that my lively sham-rocks, especially Klaus and Annemie, won't make things too difficult for you, dearest Mother. I'm enormously pleased that you, my darling children, despite your youth, can take part in the great task confronting our people. I am delighted that my Nesthäkchen is knitting so eagerly for our warriors. But I worry about my little Lotte, whom I have not seen for a year and a half. God willing I'll be with all of you soon. In my heart I'm there already. I hope to have more good news from you and from father. May my deepest love for you all reach you with this letter to Germany. May my letter finally arrive at its destination. I embrace all of you passionately.

"Your faithful daughter and mother."

There was silence, total silence, after Hans had finished reading. Grandmother wiped tears from her eyes. To the other children, it was as though Mother had finally spoken to them in her own voice.

Hans knew what it meant to his mother to be living in the enemy's country during Germany's greatest times. Every victory celebrated at home she heard about in disparaging or mendacious terms.

Nesthäkchen whispered softly, longingly, "My mommy."

Klaus was not very sentimental. The silence bothered him, and he was first to break it. "Naturally the English read our letters to mommy. That's as clear as dumpling broth. I wrote a title on every letter: 'God punish England.' Certainly they didn't want to let letters like that into the country."

Everyone laughed loudly.

"Yes, my boy, if you were so frank, it's obvious what the English would do. Anyhow, thank God we finally got a message, and Mommy is well again," said Grandmother, feeling that a burden had been lifted from her heart.

"Mommy's letter is my most beautiful Christmas gift," said Annemarie, who then turned to Grandmother a little fearfully. "Don't be offended, Grandma, but the clock you gave me didn't mean quite as much."

Grandmother assured Annemarie that she could understand how the girl would value a letter from Mommy more than any other gift. Relieved, Nesthäkchen went to her room to get dressed. Everyone else did too.

In past years, Annemarie played with her toys on Christmas Day, or read the books she had received. Today there was something else to read.

Annemarie sat re-reading Mommy's letter the whole morning. By noon she knew it by heart. Soon it would be forwarded to father.

"Grandma, do you think mommy will be home before the end of the year? She wrote 'as soon as possible.' And 1915 is frightfully far off."

Grandmother was not able to give Nesthäkchen a comforting answer. She could only counsel patience and hope that mommy would be home soon.

Hope and patience may console the elderly, but the young want certainty quickly. Annemarie was in no way consoled, and she went about the house asking everyone the same question.

Fräulein had no answer. She hemmed and hawed. Annemarie took this to mean that Mother would be home by New Year's Eve.

Hanne had the opposite opinion and Nesthäkchen could not talk her out of it. "The English are not going to let any more Germans out right now, when they're so frightened that our Zeppelins are going to spit out bombs on their roofs.[1] They would be dumb if they did."

Brother Hans opined that the homecoming would occur at the beginning of the new year, as the English wouldn't allow any trains into Germany before then.

"Yeah, maybe New Year 1916," interjected Klaus. "They've interned all Germans. They're putting them in big prison camps, where the conditions are horrible, and they can't make trips home."

"Not Mommy. Mommy will live with our relatives until 1916. Anyway, the war will have been long over by then. In the meantime, Kläuschen, put five pennies in the foreign word box. *Interned* is a foreign word." Nesthäkchen pulled out her field gray box that swallowed the fines.

Klaus showed little inclination to fish in his pocket. "*Interned* is the usual word for the arrest of civilian prisoners. Every newspaper uses it," he explained patiently. "You simply don't understand."

"It's still a foreign word and you must pay," his sister insisted.

Hanne, busy housecleaning, was enlisted as referee. Her view was that one could say *locked up* as well as *interned*, but Annemarie wouldn't listen, and Kläuschen had to part with his five pennies.

---

1. During the First World War, the German military deployed 115 Zeppelins for a variety of missions including reconnaissance and bombing, despite their vulnerability to attack and bad weather. Zeppelin aircraft were removed from front line service at Verdun in 1916, as improved Allied aircraft succeeded in achieving a high destruction rate. Newer models were later introduced that could fly higher, although this diminished their bombing accuracy. Zeppelin use was more or less discontinued in 1917 as Allied bombers demonstrated a consistent ability to destroy them.

CHAPTER 13

▼

GOOD PERFORMANCE

As Annemarie read her mother's letter again and again, she began thinking of other things besides the return journey. Didn't mommy write that her Lotte should use all her strength to take care of Grandma?

Nesthäkchen blushed. Had she ever thought that Grandma was her responsibility? She had formerly accepted all Grandmother's love and sacrifice as her due. Annemarie never once considered the idea that the converse might apply, that is, that she had obligations to Grandmother. Grandmother, despite her advanced age, had given up peace and comfort to care for her grandchildren. Mother's words had opened Nesthäkchen's eyes.

And what about the next sentence in mommy's letter? Weren't Annemarie and Klaus making Grandma's task more difficult. Annemarie was honest enough not to dispute this point. How often Grandma had worried about the itinerant Klaus' whereabouts. How often the elderly lady had called out behind the two siblings, "Children, please do me a favor: don't slam the doors." Had Nesthäkchen tried to oblige Grandma? Of course, but only after the bang of the door had already startled the old lady. And there were a hundred other things Nesthäkchen could have done to make Grandma's life more pleasant, without taking into account all the times she had not cheerfully followed Grandma's orders. How Annemarie had growled and grumbled in an ill-bred way, when she had to do something disagreeable. Heavens! Sometimes she even contradicted Grandma!

Annemarie blushed to the roots of her blond hair at these unpleasant memories. Grandma had long ago forgiven her granddaughter, but how would mommy feel about her Nesthäkchen's behavior?

Everything was certainly going to be different from now on. Before doing anything, Annemarie would ask herself, what would mommy say? Now she would take good care of Grandma.

Grandmother couldn't understand what had happened. At lunch, Nesthäkchen was quite concerned that Grandma should have a very soft slice of roast, since old people did not have good teeth. When Grandma took a second helping, her grandchild admonished her gently that too much food could ruin her stomach. For the afternoon siesta, Annemarie dragged in blankets and sheets, as though the heated room was the North Pole. When Nesthäkchen tried to wrap Grandmother in all this bedding, the old lady, breathing heavily, threw it aside, exclaiming, "Darling, you're smothering me."

Nesthäkchen was profoundly shaken. Grandmother refused to allow her granddaughter to look after her.

Nor did the door acknowledge Annemarie's good intentions. When she tried to close it quietly, it escaped her grasp and slammed shut with a crash. So Annemarie opened it again and closed it quietly.

"You know, Grandma, I will ask Fräulein to set the coffee table in the nursery. If my four girlfriends come at noon, we will otherwise make too much noise for you," said Annemarie.

Grandmother was puzzled. During her entire life, Annemarie had never worried about making too much noise. What benign spirit had entered her? As Nesthäkchen's tender concern for Grandmother increased throughout the day, the elderly lady grew more mystified.

Punctually at four o'clock, Annemarie's four girlfriends, Margot, Marlene, Ilse, and Marianne, appeared. Annemarie had chosen to celebrate Christmas with the Young Girls' Helpers.

For an entire day, Annemarie had trimmed a dolls' Christmas tree for her "children." The tree stood in the middle of the nursery table, which had been decorated in white. Around the tree she had placed gifts for her friends. Among the items were carefully crocheted blue wool booties, a hand-knitted white cap, two jackets she had crocheted during the handwork hour, and a little wooden stall with a strutting, crowing rooster.

The four girls were quite surprised. Each of them had brought a gift for an East Prussian refugee child. Margot had sewed a half dozen diapers herself. Marianne had knitted a night jacket. Ilse and Marlene together had sewn a frock, which Fräulein Hering had cut out for them. This clothing would surely have surprised any tiny refugee.

Truly the Christmas table looked enchanting. The five girls regarded their work with pride. Then they began eating chocolate and Christmas stollen, because "diligence must be rewarded," as Grandmother said. Hans and Klaus appeared and showed comparable industry depleting the mountain of pastry.

Klaus also enjoyed himself by secretly launching Puck at Margot. As big as she was, she still feared dogs. "Where is Margot? Get her, Puck, get her," Klaus whispered in the dog's ear.

In the lively din that five girls can create, no one noticed the rascally Klaus. But all of a sudden Margot emitted a shrill howl of terror, jumped from her chair, and spilled her cup of chocolate over the coffee table and Puck's white fur.

"That repulsive dog, he bit me, he bit me," cried Margot tearfully.

Poor Puck, who had only sniffed Margot's dress, had no idea what had happened to him. His friend Annemarie scolded him and chased him out of the room. Klaus, the real miscreant, enjoyed his cake with an innocent face.

"Yes, yes, that's life," thought the little dog as he licked the spilt chocolate from his fur. "Petty thieves are hanged, big ones go free."

After Margot had calmed down, Fräulein straightened up the room. Annemarie inquired about the well being of Grandmother, and whether her nerves were holding out. The children finished the pitcher of chocolate and devoured the remaining pastry. Then the four girls went downstairs to the porter's quarters.

They were very disappointed. The Young Girls' Helpers' child should certainly open his eyes when his benefactresses visited. But he slept soundly.

"Will he wake up soon, Frau Kulicke?" asked one of the foster mothers.

"It's impossible to know. If Mäxchen wants, he often sleeps until eight and then screams the whole night."

That was not encouraging. They wouldn't be able to give Mäxchen anything. All five girls had to be home by eight PM.

As hostess and former foster mother, Annemarie suggested a solution.

"Maybe we can wake him up?"

"No—*Good heavens,* no! There's no way to shut him up. He'll howl until early morning, non-stop," said Frau Kulicke with horror in her eyes.

Aw, the boy would stop crying immediately when he saw the wonderful gifts the girls had brought.

When the porter's wife went into the kitchen, Annemarie plucked the tiny nose of the sweetly slumbering infant. He growled in his sleep, but did not awaken.

Annemarie tried harder.

"Boy, wake up, we have Christmas gifts for you," screamed Nesthäkchen into the child's wagon. The four other girls stood anxiously by.

The offering made no impression on the diminutive sleeper.

Was there no wet sponge here? Annemarie remembered that Fräulein awakened her with a few drops from a sponge during her first school years, when nothing else worked.

No sponge was to be found. But there was a half-filled watering can nearby, with which Frau Kulicke tended her flowers.

"No, Annemarie, no, don't do it!" cried Margot terrified. She had a younger sister and knew that a sleeping infant should never be disturbed.

"Ah, what the heck, only a few drops," said Nesthäkchen, watering can in hand.

Gracious—instead of a few drops, a cataract drenched the unsuspecting infant.

Jolted from his sleep, Mäxchen screamed loudly, although he was no more startled than Annemarie herself. This was a catastrophe she had not foreseen.

The four other girls were shocked.

Luckily, Frau Kulicke was accustomed to the child's screams, and remained quietly in her kitchen. Nesthäkchen tried to dry the dripping Mäxchen with her handkerchief, but he continued to screech angrily.

"We'll wrap him in that big tablecloth and take him upstairs. He'll stop screaming there," suggested Annemarie, whose bad conscience was prodding her to vacate the porter's apartment forthwith.

No sooner said than done.

The girls wrapped Max warmly in the tablecloth they had brought along, and turned the pillowcases inside out so that their moisture would not attract attention. Then the caravan got under way, Annemarie at its head carrying the infant, whom the swaddling had somewhat quieted.

Max had gotten quite heavy in the past few weeks. Deathly afraid of dropping the flailing baby, the girls passed him from one to another until they reached the Braun apartment.

Pandemonium erupted. The whole family, including Hanne and Puck, ran in, wondering what had happened.

The five girls began singing *Silent Night,* trying to introduce Max to the solemn rituals of Christmas.

Max was in no mood for ceremony. He shut his eyes and contorted his brow, as though he didn't want to see anything, while opening his mouth and shrieking more vociferously than before in an honest effort to drown out *Silent Night*.

It made no difference that Annemarie showed him the bright blue booties she had crocheted, or that Margot held out the diapers she had sewn. The ungrateful brat screamed unceasingly.

Annemarie broke out in a cold sweat.

Grandmother had to summon up her pity again. She tried thumping her foot and clapping to quiet the infant. "Heavens, his little jacket is soaked. How can the woman leave a child lying like this. He'll catch his death," she said, shaking her head.

Annemarie blushed. Her four friends giggled.

"I wanted to spray him a little, so he would wake up, but all the water in the watering can splashed him," said Annemarie after some hesitation.

"What, you woke the poor sleeping kid with a watering can? He has every right to scream," said Grandmother, not knowing whether to laugh or become annoyed.

The girls changed Mäxchen's clothes. He got a new jacket and the bright blue booties. Alas, he didn't appreciate their value and put them immediately in his mouth.

At least he became friendlier. There was only one further flare-up. When Annemarie allowed her toy crowing rooster to perform for him, Max started crowing much louder than the rooster had.

The Young Girls' Helpers rejoiced heartily when Fräulein carried the pint-sized screamer back to the porter's apartment and sought a dry place to deposit him. Now the girls were able to disport themselves without impediment until they had to go home.

After saying goodnight, Nesthäkchen asked whether the shrieking infant had been hard on Grandmother's nerves. The old lady was able to restrain her curiosity no longer, and asked, "Tell me, darling, why are you so worried about me today? I'm not accustomed to such solicitude."

"Mommy wrote that I should look after you, Grandma," said Nesthäkchen abashed.

Yes, even a mother in London could have her wishes carried out in Berlin.

CHAPTER 14

▼

STRETCH YOUR SUPPLIES!

The Great War year 1914 was over, and 1915 stormed upon the world, no less warlike or saber-rattling. Millions of Germans received the New Year with optimism. Everyone hoped that the mighty victories of 1914 would be consolidated and bring an honorable peace.

As though the New Year knew what everyone wanted, the joy of victory visited the German people in February. Hindenburg, the savior of the eastern borderlands, waged a powerful nine-day battle in the Masurian Lake District, driving the Cossacks from East Prussia forever.[1]

---

1. The Second Battle of the Masurian Lakes (Winter Battle of the Masurian Lakes) opened during a severe blizzard, February 7, 1915, and formed part Paul von Hindenburg's plan for a two-pronged decisive push against the Russian Army by the Austrians and Germans. Hindenburg aimed to force Russia's defeat and so bring about an end to war on the Eastern Front. Specifically, he intended to outflank Russian positions in central Poland, and push the Russians back beyond the Vistula River. Hindenburg's plan called for the deployment of two German armies in East Prussia—the Eighth and Tenth—against the Russian Tenth Army. The Russians were defeated and in disorderly retreat by 14 February. They had suffered 56,000 casualties during the engagement. German losses were relatively small. Hindenburg's forces captured 100,000 Russian prisoners.

Colorful victory banners fluttered from the houses of Berlin, while victory pride surged and billowed in the wind. Black, white and red flags, black and yellow flags, and Turkish half-moon flags hung everywhere, even from the Braun's balcony. All of the three Braun children had hung a different colored flag. Ever since the Turks had become Germany's ally, Klaus had chosen the Turkish banner for himself.[2] Because of her love for the fatherland, Annemarie did not want the black, white, and red banner of the Austrian ally. Hans accepted it.

Rejoicing children celebrated every victory with banners and school holidays. Dr. Braun's offspring had varied reactions. Hans was most interested in the military aspects. Klaus, who was quite lazy, wondered whether a military victory would lead to the cancellation of classes. Nesthäkchen waited for a victory that the English would consider important enough to allow Mommy to come home.

She waited in vain. Now the family was regularly receiving Mrs. Braun's cards and letters, but that was all.

"Grandmother," Nesthäkchen said passionately, "I think the meanest thing the English have done is not to let Mommy out. But our school principal says they are even meaner. They want to starve German women and children to death, and only because they are so angry about our submarines and Zeppelins. The principal says they will never succeed. Each of us must help to ruin this shameful plan. From now on, I will eat two slices of bread and butter, no more, at dinner, even if I am still hungry. For breakfast, no buttered rolls, just bread and marmalade. It is absolutely necessary that we stretch our supplies, according to our school principal, and every child who loves the fatherland must make sacrifices."[3]

"Oh, darling, it won't be as bad as you think," said Grandmother, smiling at Annemarie's earnestness. "I think you can eat all you want. We have a lot of grain in Germany."

"Next month we are getting bread ration cards, so there can't be as much bread as you think," said Klaus. "Our teacher told us seriously that we must use grain sparingly and pull our belts a bit tighter."

---

2. Turkey signed a secret treaty August 2, 1914, allying itself with Germany and Austria (the Central Powers) but this agreement was not made public until October 29th.
3. At the outbreak of war in August 1914, the British used their fleet to clamp a naval blockade on Germany, cutting off many vital imports, including food.

"Hanne, our cupboard will soon be bare," said Grandmother half-jokingly. "Maybe it would be good if we set aside some provisions. We should buy more hulled fruits and flour."

"No, Grandmother, you shouldn't do that," said Annemarie with agitation. "Fräulein Drehmann said that anyone who hoards supplies sins against the fatherland."

But Grandmother was as practical as she was patriotic. Her favorite proverb was, care in time of plenty will provide for us in time of need. She could see nothing wrong in bringing home a pound of flour, rice, or gruel when she went shopping. She would see to it that her grandchildren never went hungry.

The grandchildren nevertheless felt pride in the fatherland and were determined to impose deprivations on themselves. At dinner Hans scraped away the ample layer of butter Grandmother had spread on his bread, declaring, "Fat will become scarce; one doesn't need to eat it smeared so thickly," at which point Klaus and Annemarie asked for two more slices of buttered bread.

"Klaus, you must still be hungry," said Fräulein. "Ordinarily, five slices of buttered bread don't fill you up," she added, having missed Hans' hunger declaration.

"Naturally I'm hungry, incredibly hungry, but I won't eat another piece of buttered bread. Better I should have a hole in my stomach than England should force a starving Germany to accept an ignominious peace," proclaimed Klaus grandiloquently, as he fixed his famished eyes on a plate of ham and sausage.

"OK, we have ham on a roll if you don't want more buttered bread," said Grandmother smiling.

Klaus looked longingly at the food but replied, "No, no, rolls are made from grain."

"You know, Klaus, you don't want to overdo it. I think you should begin your deprivation-cure gradually," said Grandmother, since it was difficult for her not to try to fatten her grandchildren. "Today you can eat four pieces of buttered bread, instead of your usual five. Tomorrow you can eat three pieces. Hanne will cook potatoes for us to fill in the gaps." She handed the starving Klaus bread and cold cuts.

Grandmother was right, as always. Klaus chewed with bulging cheeks. But Nesthäkchen was oblivious to Grandmother's entreaties, although she enjoyed food as much as Klaus.

In fact, Nesthäkchen had made a bet with her friends. The winner would be the girl who could eat only two sandwiches for dinner, and Nesthäkchen did not want to lose.

When Fräulein entered the nursery that night, Annemarie lay restlessly in her bed, under the picture of the beach at Wittdünn.

"What's wrong, Annemie, aren't you asleep yet?" asked Fräulein.

"No," said Nesthäkchen feebly.

"Don't you feel well?" said the worried Fräulein.

"I have pains in my stomach," was the sad reply.

"Pains in your stomach? Surely you're hungry, Annemie," laughed Fräulein. "That's what happens when you don't eat enough for dinner."

"But the principal said that Germany would be starved out—"

"So you're trying starvation to see what it feels like," said Fräulein with a smile. "Certainly your principal didn't mean for you to do that, child. He was warning about unnecessary use of grain, which should not be wasted or consumed profligately. You can still enjoy your three pieces of buttered bread, Annemie."

"Do you really mean that, Fräulein?" said Nesthäkchen doubtfully. But she reached eagerly into the cookie tin that Fräulein brought to her.

"If you don't eat these, you will have starved by the time I wake up in the morning, Annemiechen."

"Oh, beloved, golden Fräulein, I had such fear that I will have starved by the time mommy gets home. Now I'm much better. My tummy pains are gone." With her stomach full, Nesthäkchen fell asleep.

Next day, Annemarie announced to her friends that she was the only one who had eaten two sandwiches for the fatherland, because cookies were not grain.

"Anyone who brings buttered bread and meat to school is unpatriotic," said Annemarie loudly during recess, with a meaningful glance at Vera, who was standing alone in the corner.

Vera, about to bite into a piece of bread and sausage, laid down her food terrified. When she got home, Vera begged her aunt not to give her bread with meat to take with her to school. How contemptuously Annemarie Braun had stared at her.

Annemarie's Christmas Eve sympathy for Vera had long since evaporated. It's not easy to bring a rolling wheel to a stop, especially if you were the person who gave the wheel its first push, as Annemarie had. If she should suddenly change her attitude toward Vera, what would the other girls think? She would be conceding that she had done the wrong thing. Her pride would not allow her to make such a concession. But it was a false pride that prevented Doctor's Nesthäkchen from acting on the good impulses in her heart.

Annemarie was aware of this fact. She felt remorse when she saw the sadness in Vera's eyes. During recess, Vera stood isolated and abandoned, while the other girls chatted happily and romped about. Yet Nesthäkchen silenced the burdensome voice that whispered to her, "You see that? That is your work," with a defiant, "She is still a spy."

When the bread ration cards were introduced, Hans weighed each bread slice with painstaking precision on a letter scale, determined that no one should consume a gram more bread than was his allotment.

"Hanne, your buttered bread is much too thick. You alone eat one hundred fifty grams at dinner. How will you stretch your bread allotment to fill the whole day?" Hans asked the cook.

But Hanne gave as good as she got.

"I want to tell you something, young man. I don't eat grams. I eat my buttered bread. May the devil take whatever it weighs. If anybody says I'm not patriotic, I say, my little savings I'll gladly sacrifice for the fatherland and our soldiers. But my buttered bread—well, the English can go hang."

"But Hanne, you're not saving food for the English. It's for our German women and children that we must stretch our supplies," said Hans. Every day Hans gave the kitchen fairy the same lecture if she had used too much fat in the food. Every day he was equally unsuccessful. Hanne impatiently turned her broad back to him.

The impudent Klaus ribbed Hanne. "If anybody discovers a bigger gun than our forty-two centimeter mortar, they won't call it the *Fat Bertha*. They'll call it the *Fat Hanne*, in your honor.[4]

Grandmother didn't like the bread ration cards either. Age accepts change much less readily than youth. She had always kept plenty of food around, and

---

4. Produced by the German firm of Krupp, the Big Bertha (called Fat Bertha in German and French) was a 42cm howitzer, model L/14, designed in the aftermath of the Russo-Japanese War of 1904 for the German Army. The unflattering name came from association with the wife of Gustav Krupp, owner of the Krupp factory. Her name was Bertha Krupp von Bohlen und Halbach. The Big Bertha was initially used to demolish the fortresses of Liege and Namur in August 1914. It was thereafter employed to similarly reduce other enemy strong points. Only four Big Bertha howitzers were produced, the first two finished a few days after the onset of hostilities, on 9 August 1914. The huge guns, weighing some 820kg each, were shipped disassembled to their destination point, where a crew of as many as 1,000 men once again reassembled them. With a range of 15km their 42 cm shells proved devastating. All four guns were enlisted during the German assault upon Verdun from February 1916. Once the Verdun offensive was called off in failure (leading to the replacement of German Chief of Staff Erich von Falkenhayn who had initiated the battle) the Big Bertha guns were decommissioned, since Allied artillery developments had resulted in guns with a longer range. After World War I, a Big Bertha was put on display in the Museum of Military History (Heeresgeschichtliches Museum) in Vienna. In 1942, the Germans dragged the gun off to Stalingrad, and it was never seen again.

now she couldn't buy as much bread as she wanted. Indeed, bread soon became scarce in the house, because Klaus' stomach gradually forgot all about patriotism, and proceeded to fill itself with five slices of bread and butter at dinner, as it always had. Grandmother was able to forego bread much more easily than her grandchildren, but being forced to weigh each piece of bread and portion of flour was a fearful experience for her. And Hans drove himself crazy weighing and calculating amounts in grams.

What a time this was. Often Grandmother felt that she didn't fit in any longer.

Almost every week her grandchildren came home from school bringing her more worries.

"Grandma, do you still have gold?" asked Nesthäkchen one day.

"Regretfully, the war prices have melted it all together," said Grandmother jokingly.

"You can't have gold any longer, Grandma. We have to gather up all the gold in the house, bring it to school, and exchange it for paper money."

"Goodness, even in my dreams I never thought that would happen," exclaimed Grandmother.

A provident and fearful woman, Grandmother had set aside as much gold as she could. Gold always retains its value, even when paper money becomes worthless. Now she was supposed to give up her gold? That would be more than foolish.

But Grandmother had not reckoned with the persistence and eloquence of her three grandchildren. What's dear to one person is cheap to another. Klaus went trumpeting through the house, "Anyone who doesn't turn her gold into the Reichsbank betrays the fatherland." Hans gave endless daily lectures on the importance of putting all gold in the service of the state. Grandmother gradually softened up. Then Nesthäkchen delivered the *coup de grâce* with her tender pleading, stroking and kissing. The little flatterer finally convinced Grandmother to take her five gold pieces to school or give them to Fräulein to do it. (Grandmother did not trust the profligate Annemarie with a hundred marks.)

The children naturally wanted to have some of the gold brought to school and exchanged. The remainder Grandmother took to the Reichsbank herself. She would never have thought that she would ever have exchanged her hoarded gold for paper. But the intelligent, patriotic woman had learned that it was necessary to set the welfare of the people above the welfare of the individual. "Yes, yes, the world has turned upside down. Now the old learn from the young," she said half seriously, half jokingly, to Aunt Albertinchen.

But when one day the three children again assaulted the household, Grandmother no longer laughed. They wanted to turn in the copper kettles, Grandmother's beautiful, voluminous kettles, which sparkled every Saturday after they had been polished.

"They'll give us an inscribed iron ring in exchange. Won't you give up a few of your old kettles, dearest only Grandma?" said Annemarie with her pleading blue eyes as she tenderly stroked Grandmother.

It wasn't easy to deny Annemarie anything or to ignore her pleading eyes. But to Grandmother this was certainly a heavy sacrifice. She had inherited the kettles, the housewife's pride, from her own mother. No! This time Grandmother put her foot down.

Next day, Annemarie came home from school crying. Even Vera brought in a copper kettle and got a souvenir ring. Nesthäkchen was the only child who hadn't. The girl's tears softened Grandmother's heart.

"OK," Grandmother sighed, "but only two little ones, no more."

"Oh, that will be enough. Certainly I'll get a ring," said Annemarie, almost crushing Grandmother with her joyous embrace. Nesthäkchen seemed to think that copper was being collected only for the purpose of delighting school children with souvenir rings.

Brother Hans set her straight.

"Souvenir rings are certainly fine, but inessential. The most important thing is that we have enough copper to produce munitions." Hans now began his lengthy lecture and it was a pity that his audience didn't stay until the end. Annemarie left after the first few words, but only to annoy Klaus, because she had gotten two kettles while he had got none.

Grandmother had become active in the economy, Hans continued, speaking to Puck, the last of the audience and the only one who seemed to value the talk.

In the nursery, a lively dispute broke out between Klaus and Annemarie.

"Of course you have to share a kettle with me, you stupid thing. One belongs to me," cried Klaus passionately.

"Not true, Grandmother gave both kettles to me. For one little kettle I won't get a ring." Was it any wonder that all of Europe was fighting, when even in Dr. Braun's nursery war had broken out? It had been a long time since the two siblings had had such a row.

"Klaus, Annemie, you should both be ashamed of yourselves," said Grandmother and Fräulein in unison, earnestly trying to bring about peace.

"That Klaus wants to steal my kettle, Grandma," cried Annemarie in tears.

"One kettle belongs to me," Klaus retorted.

"No my son, you're wrong. They both belong to me, and I have given them to Annemie," said Grandmother quietly to the belligerent parties.

"Then let me get another kettle from Hanne," said Klaus as he left the room. Naturally, Nesthäkchen followed him to recapture the offensive. But Fräulein restrained her.

Grandmother said seriously, "I care for you all joyfully, children, and I take the small discomforts and disturbances of a large household in stride. But I cannot abide disputations and wrangling. I'm too old and too accustomed to peace and quiet. If you want me to stay here, you must behave accordingly."

Annemarie blushed at Grandmother's forceful words and was immediately reminded of Mommy's letter. Did Mommy not urge her to take care of Grandma? Indeed, Annemarie had forgotten mommy's words, as she had forgotten much else.

"Forgive me, Grandma," said Annemarie ashamed. "I will remember that you're old and can't tolerate noise."

Klaus returned with a bitterly angry face. Hanne would enter into no negotiations and defended her kettles, like a lioness defends her cubs.

Without prodding, Nesthäkchen said, "I'll give you one kettle, Klaus."

"You see," said Klaus, "you could have spared us all that squabbling."

Next day Dr. Braun's offspring marched peacefully to school, each with a kettle, and both children came home with souvenir rings.

Grandmother saw the good relations between the two and thought, "If only peace would return to the world as quickly as it has to my bellicose household."

CHAPTER 15

▼

REICH WOOL WEEK

The Reich Wool Week arrived, the strangest week associated with the war. In the German Reich, rich and poor took part. Every great house and little cottage turned chests and closets inside out. Each individual gave the government old woolen garments she could do without.

"Children, I must thank God if you leave the clothes on my body," said Grandma. Truly the three grandchildren had robbed her completely. Nothing was safe from them. They didn't overlook a thing. They even confiscated the old Persian carpet. Klaus swiped the wool cloth that Hanne used for polishing and said later, with naughty piety, that it had been torn. Fräulein caught Annemarie rummaging around in the patch box. When Fräulein later wanted to repair some trousers for Hans, naturally the matching patches were missing. Nesthäkchen had consigned everything, including the patches, to the wool basket. The wool was intended for the troops, and Hans went around with a mismatched patch on his trousers.

To the rascal Annemarie, rummaging through closets and collecting long-for-gotten objects had become a party. Hans and Klaus too labored diligently during Reich Wool Week. Their schools bestowed on them and many other boys the honor of pulling a cart from house to house to collect woolen articles, always three boys to a cart. If anyone had tried to impose this task on the students before, the boys would have hated them. But now the noble gymnasium students were proud to do the work, because the British naval blockade was beginning to bite.

For the first time in her life, Annemarie was not content with her lot. Oh, if only she were a boy. When her brothers pompously displayed their daily lists of the streets to which they had been assigned, she felt envy. She ardently wished to pull the handcart too.

"Kläuschen, dearest Kläuschen, can't you take me along just this once?" Annemarie whispered pleadingly one afternoon to her brother as he was about to leave.

Instead of answering, Klaus tapped his forehead expressively. But this gesture did not impede his sister from bombarding him with more pleas.

"One time, and I'll give you the whole box of pastry Aunt Albertinchen brought yesterday," she said.

That did it. Klaus would do anything for sweets. Of course, the sly girl was well aware of this fact.

"No, I can't let you," said Klaus, suddenly changing his mind. "Girls can't come along. I would feel ashamed in front of the other boys."

"Oh, Kläuschen, I'll put on my blue gym pants, my striped sailor blouse, and I'll hide my hair under my sailor cap. I'll look just like a boy. OK? You'll take me along, Kläuschen?" said Annemarie leaping into the air.

"Grandma won't permit it—" said Klaus without much conviction, fascinated by the idea of a disguise and won over by Aunt Albertinchen's pastry.

"Oh, Grandmother is asleep. I'll be back long before she wakes up. Fräulein is visiting her wounded cousin in the military hospital. Hanne is running around looking for petroleum, it's so scarce. Not a soul will notice my absence. I'll be ready in five minutes," said Annemarie dashing off.

In a few moments an enchanting blond boy entered the room, against whom Klaus had no more objections.

"My two classmates who are coming along don't know you. I'll tell them I'm bringing along my little brother. Let's go!" Laughing and giggling the two children stormed down the steps. The two other "rag boys" were waiting with their handcart.

"My little brother," said Klaus, laughing archly. Annemarie quickly turned away her blushing face. "Come, Karlchen, we'll pull first, the cart is still very light."

Klaus and the giggling "Karlchen" began to pull, and the motley team rattled through the fashionable streets of West Berlin.

With glistening eyes Annemarie trotted along like a cart dog. Never before in her life, even on her first day of school, had she been so proud.

Luckily the boys only needed to visit nearby homes today. The two classmates went to the door with their identification, while Klaus and Annemarie watched the cart. The boys left the homes with a rich bounty—flannel underskirts, torn underwear, pieces of carpet and rags. As they left each house, the cart got gradually heavier. The pull-rope cut Nesthäkchen's hands, even though it didn't spoil her pleasure.

"What muscles that little boy has," said one of the classmates appreciatively, spurring Annemarie onward.

In the March sun, a woman on the street approached the caravan. Annemarie looked at her closely. Holy cow! It was Fräulein Neubert, the strictest teacher in the Schubert Girls' Lyceum. "If only she doesn't recognize me."

Fräulein Neubert approached more closely. She looked on with interest, as had the other passersby. A team of youthful rag collectors in the upscale streets of Berlin was an unusual sight.

Annemarie almost turned her head off her neck, so sharply had she twisted it in the opposite direction. What would happen if Fräulein Neubert recognized her? What should she do if Fräulein Neubert rebuked her tomorrow, because she had not said hello? With her heart pounding, Annemarie squinted sideways. In doing so she met Fräulein Neubert's eyes and, wonder of wonders: The picture-pretty boy, to the astonishment of Fräulein Neubert and the other onlookers, executed a mannerly curtsy.

Klaus gave his sister an annoyed thump. "What will the boys think of you? You must raise your hat when you greet someone."

Right! Nesthäkchen in her excitement hadn't thought of that, or about now being "Karlchen."

The two classmates were behind the cart, watching that nothing got lost or stolen, and luckily had not noticed the strange greeting.

"So, Braun, now you and your little brother have to visit the houses. We all take turns," said one of the classmates as the cart turned into a new street.

Braun and his "little brother" got under way.

In the first house they entered, everything went quickly. The one tenant had already given assorted woolens to the landlord, who gave them to the children. But at the next house they went up and down steps empty handed.

Most people were friendly toward the two youngsters. Some, however, saw them as tiresome beggars and slammed the door in their faces.

The sensitive Annemarie was almost in tears.

"Look, Klaus," said Annemarie, pulling timidly at her brother's sleeve as he was about to ring the bell of the apartment across the hall, "If we get tossed out again, I'm not doing this with you any more."

"Do what you want. For our soldiers, we can be thrown out and accept it calmly."

The lady in the next home received the two children kindly.

"Please come in, you can take the things right away. They're ready for you in the next room. Can you carry everything, my son?" said the lady, patting Annemarie amicably on the cheek as she led the siblings to a small sunny balcony room, where a young boy pored over his schoolbooks. As he lifted his head, Nesthäkchen happily yelled, "Kurt—Kurt!"

"Annemarie, is it really you?" he replied delighted. "This is Annemarie Braun. I was with her in the children's sanatorium at Wittdünn and traveled home with her," he told his mother.

The mother looked at the beaming girl, whom she had called "my son."

"Kurt told me a lot about you, and it sounded as though you were always half-boy. Now have you become a whole boy?" she said jokingly, glancing at Annemarie's trousers.

"No, no, I was so frightfully anxious to go wool-collecting with Klaus—this is my brother Klaus," stuttered a confused Annemarie.

"I always believed you would come visit me, Annemarie. You promised me you would. But I thought you had completely forgotten me," said Kurt a bit reproachfully.

"Yes, what with the war, I did forget, Kurt," admitted Nesthäkchen. "And I haven't written to Gerda Eberhard in Breslau, who was so friendly with me in Wittdünn." Annemarie was always forgetting something.

"Next Sunday you must come to visit my Kurt. I'm so happy he has some old friends," said the mother.

Klaus and Annemarie said thank you and left with their bundle of wool, Kurt accompanying them to the door on two crutches.

"You still can't walk, Kurt?" Annemarie asked the limping boy compassionately.

He shook his head. "I was better in Wittdünn. But I still feel lucky when I see on the street the pathetic soldiers with no legs. Anyway, *auf Wiedersehen* until Sunday."

Kurt waved from the balcony at Klaus and Annemarie.

The wool gathering continued house to house. Annemarie met friendly and unfriendly people during her wanderings. A fat butcher took off wool clothing he was wearing and handed it to her: "Oh, what, take my rags with you, boys, our soldiers need them more than I do."

The bartender on the corner invited Annemarie to have "a few drops," then handed her an enormous foaming beer stein, commenting, "this will put some hair on your chest, my boy."

The beer was fun, but the woolen rags were not as appetizing. Annemarie passed two wool horse blankets deftly to Klaus. They were too much for her sensitive nose but didn't bother him as much.

"So, now for the last house, then we can turn all this stuff in," said Klaus as he pulled Annemarie along.

"We won't get anything here. These are very elegant people," said Nesthäkchen as she spied the doorplate.

"Von Hohenfeld, Royal Governmental Counselor," read Klaus.

The maid opened the door. The entry hall was decorated with flowers.

"This is a noble family," said Annemarie as the maid handed her the woolen scraps.

Two deep blue youthful eyes stared at the wool gatherers through a crack in the door. Annemarie's heart began to pound. She knew those eyes. What was the Polack doing in this fine home?

Vera recognized Annemarie immediately, despite her odd costume. A gleam of happiness appeared in Vera's gorgeous pale face as she pulled open the door and hurried out.

"Annemarie," said Vera, still unable to pronounce the guttural German *rrrr*, "have you come to visit me?" Vera happily held both arms out to the girl who had treated her so contemptuously and had made her a pariah in school.

Annemarie was painfully embarrassed. The usually outspoken Nesthäkchen was unable to utter a word.

Vera's aunt, Mrs. von Hohenfeld, appeared in the doorway. Klaus tipped his hat politely, and, following her brother's example, Annemarie did the same. Amazed, the lady stared at the pretty boy with two blond pigtails.

"You're here for the woolens, children? I plundered my whole moth-proof-chest. Take everything for our brave warriors," said Mrs. von Hohenfeld as she handed over her woolens and Vera whispered in her ear, "Aunt—Aunt—that's Annemarie Braun, from my class."

"Oh, a classmate. Our Vera would love to visit with you. Stay awhile if you have time, my child," said the wife of the Royal Governmental Counselor to the blushing Annemarie.

Nesthäkchen wished she were on the other side of the world. But since this wish would never be fulfilled, she answered, "I can—*achoo!*" The moth-proof-chest, in which the woolens lay, was asserting itself. "I really can't—*achoo! achoo!*—many thanks, but my grandmother is waiting—*achoo!*" The sneezing impeded Annemarie's expression of regret.

"Will you come visit me soon?" said Vera with urgency in her deep blue eyes. "Yes, will you come?'

"*Achoo! Achoo!*" was the only answer Vera received.

Annemarie tipped her hat to Mrs. von Hohenfeld, curtseyed in a confused way, and hastened from the room.

Nesthäkchen didn't like to lie. There was no chance she would ever come to visit Vera. Nor would she ever permit Vera to visit her. Absolutely not. With disappointment in her eyes, Vera heard Annemarie's parting remark from the front steps: "*Achoo!*"

"That's your Polack? Those people are high nobility," said Klaus at the foot of the stairs. "She doesn't look like any spy to me. Not with an uncle who's a royal governmental counselor."

"Excuse me," said Annemarie defensively, "you were the one who first accused her of being a spy."

"Hmmm—well, it's still possible," said Klaus, who was not entirely cured of his spy mania. "Since her uncle is a member of the government, she has an ideal setup for espionage."

"She's going to wait a long time before I'll ever visit her. I wouldn't care if she lived in a palace. Just wait and see how that Polack will use her opportunity to avenge herself on me. She'll blab to everyone in class that I'm running around in trousers. Because of the stupid Vera I have no desire to do any more wool collecting with you. Anyhow, I have to get home. It's almost four," said Annemarie.

"Nonsense, early tomorrow morning it'll be four again. Now it's almost five," said Klaus, pointing at a tower clock that began to strike the hour.

"Almighty chocolate—Grandmother is waiting for me. I must rush home. Goodbye!"

"Goodbye, Karlchen," rang out three voices behind the hurrying girl.

Annemarie had no need to hurry. Although it was five o'clock, Grandmother had not noticed that Annemarie was missing. She hadn't even thought to ring for coffee, though the coffee hour had long passed.

Unmoving, the elderly lady sat and stared at the letter in her hand, which had just arrived. It was from her daughter in England.

"Dear God, how will I tell the children?" thought Grandmother.

She heard Nesthäkchen's bright voice ringing through the house. A few minutes later, dressed again as a girl, Annemarie entered the room.

"Please, don't be angry, Grandma," she began, looking at Grandmother shyly without noticing the letter. Was Grandmother annoyed because Nesthäkchen was home so late?

Annemarie saw the letter in Grandmother's hand.

"A letter from mommy? Hurrah! When is mommy coming home? Soon?" said Annemarie, staring hopefully at the letter.

How difficult it was to disappoint the child.

"Mommy won't be home anytime soon," said Grandmother struggling for words. Even the inexperienced Nesthäkchen knew something was very wrong. "Mommy was arrested because of a careless remark."

Nesthäkchen looked at Grandmother incredulously.

"Arrested? Under arrest? Who arrested my mommy? Why?" Annemarie's beating heart seemed to stand stock still with fear.

"The English, darling. Mommy made enthusiastic comments about the success of our submarines. Somebody overheard, and she was arrested as a spy."

"A spy—my mommy a spy!" screamed Nesthäkchen at the top of her voice as she broke out in a flood of tears.

"Be calm, darling, relax—don't get so upset, my dearest one," said Grandmother weakly, though she herself was in need of encouragement. "They'll find out that their suspicions are groundless, then they'll release her. Don't cry like that, my child," said Grandmother with tears streaming from her eyes.

Annemarie continued to sob.

Her dearly beloved mommy was in prison, as a spy. A thought popped into Annemarie's head. Was—was she responsible? Was almighty God punishing her for suspecting Vera was a spy? Was He showing her how much pain such suspicion could cause? Nesthäkchen's tears grew hotter.

Klaus came home and crashed through the house, unsuspecting. "Karlchen, where are you hiding?" It seemed to Annemarie as though it had been weeks, not hours, since she was "Karlchen" happily pulling the wool cart.

"Oh my, what happened?" said Klaus, eyebrows comically arched, to his sobbing sister.

"Mommy—my mommy," she cried, unable to say more.

Grandmother had to recount the painful news.

Klaus didn't scream or cry, as Annemarie had. He balled his fists, as though he wanted to pummel an invisible foe. "God punish England!" he exclaimed in impotent rage.

The two siblings, so recently lively, sat together completely shattered as they read their mother's letter, which consisted of only a few lines:

> "My dear ones at home! I must inflict pain on you today, and the pain is worse for me than for you. I am no longer with our relatives. I carelessly expressed my enthusiasm about the successes of our submarines all too loudly to cousin Annchen. Other people heard me and I was probably made into an example. The result was my arrest as a presumed spy. It's not too bad for me here. I hope to God that my innocence will be proven and that I will be released."

With horror in his high-spirited brown eyes, Klaus interrupted the reading, saying "If only they don't shoot mommy as a spy."

"Klaus—" screamed Nesthäkchen in pain before fainting dead away.

When she came to, Annemarie lay in her bed. By her side sat dear Grandmother with a worried face. Fräulein came and went, with cold compresses for the girl's forehead.

"Grandma, was I having a terrible dream or—is it true, Grandma…tell me, please, please, tell me that it isn't true—" said Annemarie, anxiously squeezing Grandmother's hand.

"It is unhappily the truth, my darling. But what Klaus said was stupid. No one is convicted on suspicion. Uncle John will see that mommy is released soon."

"Do you mean that truly, Grandma?" said Nesthäkchen, closing her eyes with relief. Deep relaxation followed the frightful excitement.

Though her confident words quieted the child, the old lady did not believe them in her heart. The German submarines were sinking huge numbers of ships. Zeppelins and planes were dropping bombs nightly on the English people, who were very embittered. In the big cities there were riots against German families and companies. Could enmity and animosity transform the harmless remarks of her daughter, so that an ominous future awaited her?

"Dear God above, have pity on us," prayed Grandmother.

CHAPTER 16

▼

NESTHÄKCHEN ATONES
FOR AN INJUSTICE

A golden spring engulfed the country, pouring hope into people's hearts, especially the children's. Everything in nature was renewed. How could sad thoughts persist amidst the sprouting and blooming? The spring wind blew cares and worries away.

Klaus and Annemarie felt the power of spring. After a few days of sorrow, the joy and hope of youth awoke within them. Everything had not been lost. Perhaps Mother had already been released. It took so long for a letter to reach Berlin. Why hang your head when there was no reason to do so?

The frightful calm that pervaded the Braun household for many days gradually gave way to the usual lively scene. Klaus was again crashing through the house. Nesthäkchen sang and danced. Only occasionally the children looked so thoughtful that the dear spring sunshine had difficulty making them jolly.

Hans, who since October had been in his eighth year of secondary school, had suffered most as a result of the evil letter. But very quietly, within himself. No one noticed how deeply he had been affected. As the oldest, he used all his strength to give Grandmother moral support during the difficult days. Only once he exploded.

"If Father would allow me to enlist. Two boys from my class are already at the front. If I could fight the English, I would make them pay with their blood for every tear mommy has shed."

Grandmother was shocked. What had the war done to this gentle boy?

At Easter Nesthäkchen had been put into the fifth class as second. Ilse Hermann was first. Annemarie's evaluations had been excellent, but had given her no pleasure, despite the theater tickets to *William Tell,* which Grandmother had presented to her and Klaus. If only Daddy and Mommy could have rejoiced over their diligent "Lotte," but…

Nesthäkchen had already learned during these months of war that people had to make sacrifices. But being accustomed to good luck, Annemarie thought she was somehow making bigger sacrifices than anyone else. The fathers of all her classmates were at the front, but their mothers were at home. Yet she had had to do without Father and Mother, while fearing for Mother's life.

Annemarie had never forgotten Klaus' words. They twitched in her heart and stung her, often in the middle of class, most frequently when her gaze fell upon Vera. She regretted the pain her unfounded suspicions had caused the innocent girl whenever she thought of her imprisoned mother. Hadn't she done Vera the same injustice that the English had done her own mother?

Phooey—Annemarie was a German girl and proud of it.

"Repent, it is never too late to atone," said a disagreeable voice that pointed out the right thing to do. Annemarie had the best of intentions but—being good was so difficult. She dreaded being forced to admit to her classmates that she had done an injustice.

Yet Vera was the only person in class who, Annemarie had to admit, suffered more than she herself. To Annemarie everyone was friendly and agreeable. Vera was avoided and rejected. No mother, no homeland. In comparison to Vera, Annemarie had a happy life.

Moreover, Annemarie had to admit that the "Polack" was not lusting for revenge. She never said a word in class about Annemarie in trousers. Vera's only response came the day after Annemarie and Klaus had visited Vera's aunt's house. With her pleading eyes, Vera looked at Annemarie, as if to say, "What have I done that makes you dislike me?"

But Annemarie, who would embrace her friend Margot, was too occupied with her own worries about her imprisoned mother. She had no time to deal with distressed Vera.

The more days that passed, the more unlikely it appeared that Annemarie would suddenly change her attitude toward Vera. Indeed, Annemarie was quite happy as the Easter holiday began. Now Vera's sad eyes did not remind Nesthäkchen daily of her wickedness.

Annemarie's twelfth birthday fell during Easter. Although she was not much inclined to celebrate, Grandmother had allowed Annemarie to invite her four schoolmates in for birthday chocolate. The child should have the same happy birthday as always.

Annemarie had also invited Kurt to her birthday party. She thought of inviting Vera and wavered for a moment. Here was an opportunity to atone for the injustice she had done. She felt this clearly. Inviting Vera would improve Vera's standing among her classmates. How Vera's sad blue eyes would light up.

Almost immediately, Annemarie had suppressed her reconciliatory urge. What kind of faces would her friends make? What effect would Vera's presence at the party have on Annemarie herself? Vera would be a bummer, to say the least. Thus Annemarie managed to ignore her virtuous impulse.

On April 9th, the birthday girl got her most beautiful gift, a letter from England addressed to Miss Annemarie Braun. Mommy was free! Besides the careless remark, the English hadn't the slightest evidence to allow them to incarcerate Mrs. Braun. To be sure, she had to report to the police every week. The bad news was that she would not be allowed to leave England in the foreseeable future.

Annemarie and the rest of the family were enormously relieved. Mother should remain quietly in England. The war would not last forever. At least her life was safe. If only she didn't end up in jail again.

At last, Nesthäkchen was able to enjoy her other birthday gifts. She had asked only for money, which she would use to buy gifts to send the men at the front. But Grandmother wanted Nesthäkchen to have her own gifts, although frugal ones appropriate for the time.

Annemarie was distressed that no birthday card had come from Father. As a doctor, he had been assigned to duty in the trenches, so it was probable that his card was delayed.

From Gerda Eberhard, her friend from Breslau in the children's sanatorium, Annemarie had received a darling letter. How nice of Gerda to remember her birthday. Gerda's father, a captain, lay wounded in a military hospital. So it wasn't a disaster that the birthday letter from Dr. Braun had not arrived punctually. At least he was healthy.

Aunt Albertinchen appeared at the party. Her diligent fingers had embroidered a lovely blouse for her favorite niece. Also a gentleman visited in the morning. He held a bouquet he would not relinquish, wore diapers and his first short baby dress, made by the Young Girls' Helpers. He behaved in a highly mannerly fashion. He didn't scream, laughed at Nesthäkchen, and told wonderful long stories that no one could understand. Grandmother called his speech "Pig Latin." Mäxchen was now nine months old.

Everyone enjoyed the afternoon chocolate. The giant war cake Hanne had baked was also popular. There was laughing, chatting, giggling, and whispering. The elderly ladies began to feel young as they took part in the festivities. Klaus was exceptional; he didn't annoy anyone. He even renounced his favorite pastime, launching Puck at fearful Margot. The presence of polite, modest Kurt had a very salutary effect on the other young people.

When the forfeits were drawn, there were heavy penalties for each forfeit, such as "stone crates," a ring with a mountainous mouth dug from a pile of flour, and other absurd items.[1]

Sometimes a forfeit was held up with the question, "What should the person do, whose forfeit I hold in my hand?"

"Accompany the Polack during the next recess," said Marianne laughing.

Annemarie's forehead became as red as the bow in her hair when she heard this comment. "No, no, say something else, I'll never do that," she replied forcefully. But nothing disturbed the festivities, not even this unsettling comment.

"It's a long time until the first day of school," thought Annemarie consolingly, trying to prevent her birthday mood from being spoilt. It was good that she had not invited Vera.

The party broke up at seven o'clock. During wartime, children's visits did not include dinner, because each family had only enough food for itself. At the Braun's, the week was especially parsimonious. On the way to buy bread, Klaus saw some other children playing war games on the street, Germans against English. His enmity for England prompted him to take sides, and during the mêlée he lost the bread ration cards. He came home covered with bruises and without any bread. As punishment, he didn't get bread and butter for a week. But Grandmother and Fräulein closed their eyes when Hans or Annemarie secretly slipped the always-hungry Klaus a piece of their own bread and butter. Because that same week there was a devastating potato shortage in Berlin.

Without dinner, but with many thank-you's and kisses, the girls said goodbye. Klaus accompanied Kurt to his house.

The doorbell rang. Had one of the partygoers forgotten something? Annemarie lunged for the door.

No, it wasn't one of her girlfriends. In the dim hallway stood a strange, bearded officer. No doubt a patient who had been very delayed.

---

1. The children are playing Pfänderspiel (*game of forfeits*). The American games *Spin the bottle* and *Truth or dare* have long since replaced Pfänderspiel at parties.

Annemarie curtseyed politely. "My father is at the front, but if you want to consult the doctor who is covering for him—"

Puck's wild howl of joy drowned out Nesthäkchen's carefully composed speech. There was laughter that sent Annemarie's blood rushing to her head. She looked more closely at the strange officer...and "Father—Daddy, my dear Daddy!" Annemarie leaped to wrap her arms around the "patient's" neck and stroked and kissed her bearded, sunburned father, who had returned home on leave.

"Is my Lotte really dumber than Puck? Doesn't she recognize her own father?" Dr. Braun held his daughter in his arms. Even when the rest of the family gathered around him joyously, he continued to embrace Annemarie. Was this his Lotte, his youngest? The twelve-year-old girl had grown almost tall enough to reach his shoulders.

Annemarie sat on Father's knee, as she had as a small child. She almost crushed him with her stormy, loving caresses. With infinite tenderness she focused all the longing for her far off parents, which had accumulated during the long months of war, upon her father.

There was still one parent missing, but at least Mother's letter, which had come today, made her absence less painful.

What a splendid birthday this had been! Nesthäkchen didn't want to go to bed. She sat on Father's knee until almost midnight. With Klaus and Hans nearby, Father recounted the pitched battle of Champagne.[2]

---

2. The Battle of Champagne, which began December 1914, was the Allies first attack on the Germans since the construction of trenches. The offensive was launched with minor attacks on 10 December 1914 at the southern edge of the Sayon salient, near Perthes in eastern Champagne. There was heavy fighting at Givenchy from 18-22 December, Perthes on 20 December, and at Noyon on 22 December, but French gains were minimal. The Germans were well entrenched, and successfully demonstrated the superiority of the then state of defensive warfare, especially in their use of the machine gun. Fighting continued without break until mid-February, when there was a brief lull in the battle to re-organize. Hostilities continued until 17 March 1915, when the French called off the entire offensive because of the strength of German counteroffensive, combined with a costly lack of success. Perthes had in particular seen much action, with an additional three battles being fought for its possession. The French had made minor territorial gains across the line and the French Fourth Army had made progress on the hills of eastern Champagne. But at no point did the French advance more than 3 km. French casualties numbered some 90,000; the German Third Army lost an equivalent number.

Figure 8. Annemarie leaped to wrap her arms around the "patient's" neck and stroked and kissed her bearded, sunburned father, who had returned home on leave.

"Despite all their preparations, the French couldn't break through our lines. They never will. We'll hold out," said Dr. Braun earnestly.

"Oh, Father, if I could only help. Let me join up. Two boys in my class have been in the army since October. And one boy from the class ahead of me has been killed," said Hans with blazing eyes and hot cheeks.

"No, my son, you can't convince me. You are not strong enough. Do I want to see the enemy exhaust my oldest boy? Wouldn't that be a disgrace? Ask me again in a year. God grant that we will have been victorious by then. Until that time, do your duty at home, as you have been."

Hans' heart was heavy. Grandmother breathed a sigh of relief.

"Is my Lotte asleep?" said Father, raising the blond head of his youngest child. No, she wasn't even dozing. With wide eyes she was listening to everything and basking in the joy of nestling her cheek on Father's breast.

"It's time for bed, children. Tomorrow is another day. Lotte, I must convey to you greetings and best wishes from Nurse Lenchen." Father stood up.

"Nurse Lenchen—who is that?" asked Annemarie.

"Lotte, I think you're sleeping with your eyes open," laughed Father. "First my dumb Lotte doesn't know her own father and now she doesn't remember Aunt Lenchen, who took care of her for a year at Wittdünn."

"Oh, Aunt Lenchen. Is she in the military hospital, Father?" Annemarie had been sleepy, but now she was wide-awake.

"No, child, but she is working in a first aid station, taking care of Uncle Heinrich. He was wounded, but thank God, only lightly. When she heard about me, she told me how she had looked after you. It's a small world."

"Uncle Heinrich was in Russia. How did he get to the west?" asked Hans astonished.

"The army has moved an enormous number of troops from east to west because of the huge French offensive. Uncle Heinrich came through Berlin. He wasn't able to get in touch with you, since the troop movements are secret. He even had to tell his wife and children not to come to Breslau.

"But now, good night. Oh, you don't know the wonderful feeling to be home again in your own bed," said Father.

Next morning black, white, and red banners fluttered from Dr. Braun's balcony in the spring breeze. Passersby listened hopefully for an extra edition or the ringing of bells, announcing a victory, but nothing happened. What were all the banners for? People scratched their heads. Nobody knew the answer. A joyous child's heart was expressing pleasure over Father's return from the front in the most exalted manner, the display of victory banners.

Nesthäkchen no longer strolled with Father holding his hand. With incomparable joy she took his arm on the Berlin streets. Annemarie wouldn't allow him to go anywhere by himself. She and Puck were like faithful shadows.

She accompanied him to his clinic, where two years ago she had lain for weeks with scarlet fever. The clinic was now a military hospital. Annemarie went from bed to bed distributing oranges, chocolate, and cigars. Even the wounded who were in considerable pain smiled at the happy, energetic blond girl.

Oh, why did the stupid school have to begin again? In former days Annemarie would have rejoiced to enter a new class. Now she was less thrilled. School was robbing her of two mornings and an entire afternoon with Father during his short military leave. In three days he had to return to the front.

School had another distinctly unpleasant aspect. What would happen if Marianne Davis remembered the silly chit exchanges and told people that Annemarie was supposed to accompany the Polack during recess? Annemarie would be mortally embarrassed in front of Vera. She would never accompany Vera anywhere. No, certainly not.

Annemarie begged her father to come to school with her, and not only to be with him as much as possible. Annemarie's vanity informed her plea. She wanted the schoolchildren to see her father, of whom she was so proud, with his Iron Cross. Especially Vera.

Father came to school but Vera was initially nowhere to be found.

"My father is on leave. If you look out the window right away, you'll still be able to see him. He brought me to school," Nesthäkchen said on entering her new class.

Dear me, the girls were so quiet and made comical faces. Some went to the window, but most whispered to one another or stared shyly in the opposite direction.

Annemarie looked in the direction of their glances.

On the bench next to the last, a pale child sat dressed in mourning. Her long black locks fell upon her black dress—Vera.

When the cheerful Annemarie took in this painful scene, her joy vanished immediately. Had Vera's aunt or uncle died? Annemarie felt compelled to rush to the pale, quiet girl and console her. But before she had conquered the remains of the shameful pride that prevented her from doing so, Dr. Winter, the new teacher, entered the room.

There was no instruction today. The teacher took down the names of his pupils, announced the schedule, and distributed the textbooks.

"Annemarie Braun—father's occupation?"

"Senior military physician," she said with pleasure.

After Annemarie had answered a few more questions, the teacher called out the next name in the alphabet, Vera Burkhard.

"Father's occupation?"

"Papa is—dead." Sobbing uncontrollably, Vera pressed both her hands to her ashen face.

"Right—poor child!" The teacher approached Vera and sympathetically stroked her black hair. "I heard that your father died a hero's death for our fatherland in the Carpathian battle. You must be proud of your father. But we—I know I'm speaking for all of you in the class—we want to help our dear Vera carry this heavy burden.

The teacher called out the names of the other girls, who answered while trying to hide their ashamed faces. Furtively they looked over at the deathly white Vera.

Annemarie cried openly, tears poring like a fountain down her red cheeks. Where was her vain pride? Her rueful tears had washed it away. Vera, whom Annemarie had turned into a school pariah by denouncing her as a spy, Vera had offered up to the fatherland the supreme sacrifice, her most precious possession. What did all the little sacrifices of the other girls mean when compared to this huge, exquisitely painful one?

When the school bell struck the hour, Annemarie hurried over to Vera. Passionately she embraced the weeping Vera and kissed her pallid cheeks.

"Can you ever forgive me, Vera, for treating you so badly? So badly—you can't imagine how badly. I'm frightfully sorry. I will make it all up to you. From now on you are very dear to me. You will be my friend," whispered the weeping Nesthäkchen.

At that moment, a smile like a sunbeam appeared on Vera's earnest lips. Or was the smile in Vera's blue eyes when she looked at Annemarie? Quietly Vera extended her hand to her new friend, who had treated her so wickedly.

The other girls gathered around. As they had followed Annemarie's bad example, now they followed her good one. All of them took Vera's hand. They wanted to help her, and make up for past abuses.

Annemarie closed up Vera's notebook. Margot handed Vera her black hat. Then the two girls both took Vera by the arm and headed home.

Vera's deepest desire, for which she had prayed to almighty God for months, was finally fulfilled. The other children no longer rejected her; instead, they were invariably kind. And Annemarie, her worst enemy, had become her best friend. But at what cost! Vera did not rejoice at the price she had to pay.

Figure 9. When the school bell struck the hour, Annemarie hurried over to Vera. Passionately she embraced the weeping Vera and kissed her pallid cheeks.

During the first recess, the prophecy of the chit oracle came true. Annemarie passionately embraced the once scorned "Polack."

When Doctor Braun left for the front, Nesthäkchen bravely held back her tears. She thought of Vera. No, don't cry. Indeed, she had reason to thank God.

CHAPTER 17

▼

THE WAR CHILD

Annemarie kept her word. She thought constantly about how to atone for her injustice to Vera. With tender, loving friendship she tried to console the mourning girl and heal the wounds fate had inflicted upon her. This German girl was not at all like the Italians, who often broke promises to their friends.[1]

In Doctor Braun's household, no one was unduly hard on the faithless friend and erstwhile ally that had turned its back on Germany. Hans spewed out long discourses, which always closed with the declaration that he would immediately join the army the moment a southern front opened. Flailing his arms, Klaus wished the Italians "a sound thrashing." But Nesthäkchen thought, "If I ever again treated Vera badly, I would be worse than the Italians."

Spring became summer. Grandma had no desire to visit a spa. But Berlin schoolchildren needed to visit the countryside to commune with God and nature.

---

1. Italy entered the war against Germany and Austria after signing the secret Treaty of London, 26 April 1915. The primary Allied powers—Britain, France and Russia—were, by 1915, keen to bring neutral Italy into the war on their side. Italy drove a hard bargain, demanding extensive territorial concessions once the war had been won, including Trent, Southern Tyrol, Istria, Gorizia and Dalmatia. Despite the Allies' agreement, the terms of the secret treaty were to cause problems at the Versailles Peace Conference in 1919.

The Braun children chose to vacation at the Arnsdorf farm. They would be able to help with the harvest. And Grandmother would be able to visit her second daughter, Kätchen, whom she had not seen since she moved into the Braun home.

The siblings worked with all their strength. With cousin Elli and two boy cousins they bound the sheaves and loaded the wheat. The people were short on provisions. Anyone with strong arms was a warrior.

"Next year, children, you should get twice as many bread ration cards for your diligence," joked uncle Heinrich, who had received a few weeks leave so that his wounds would heal completely. "Especially Annemarie, who plucked a bouquet of poppies and cornflowers for Grandmother, instead of looking after the wheat. Is that love for the fatherland or not, eh?"

Annemarie turned redder than her poppies, even though Uncle Heinrich was only kidding.

"Annemarie helped very diligently during the fruit harvest," said Aunt Kätchen.

"Sure, when she ate," interjected a cousin ungallantly.

Nesthäkchen looked at Aunt Kätchen gratefully. She was especially fond of her aunt during this visit because Kätchen so resembled her mother.

Klaus, famous as a rascal after previous visits, was oddly restrained. Even in this isolated spot, the seriousness of the times could be felt. The only prank he pulled was dropping half of Aunt Kätchen's provisions into an old dry water ditch out of which he had made a wonderful front line trench. Ever since Uncle Heinrich had told the children of the high life under the earth, Klaus had wanted to become a subterranean high liver.

Amidst the harvest labor, the victory bells celebrated the fall of Warsaw.[2] The capital of Poland was in German hands. Along the entire front the enemy had been beaten and forced back.

Yet the guns thundered endlessly, while shells howled through the autumn air. East, west, south, above or below the earth, with undiminished fury the world war raged. General Mackensen's victorious army marched across the Danube toward Serbia, binding East and West.[3] Bulgaria's bold sons declared themselves allies of the Central Powers, Germany and Austria. The second winter of the war began.

---

2. After fierce fighting, the Germans entered Warsaw August 5, 1915.
3. Field Marshal August von Mackensen (1849-1945) became popular with the German public after his victorious campaigns in Serbia and Romania during World War I. Hitler invited Mackensen to many Nazi festivities, where the old soldier habitually wore his snugly fitting uniform of the Death's Head Hussars.

In October, the Schubert Girls' Lyceum settled into its old rooms. The army no longer needed to use the building as a military hospital, because enough private quarters were available.

The girls worked with new diligence. Tirelessly industrious female fingers produced Christmas gifts to delight men far from home.

One ugly, rainy November day, Margot, Vera, and Annemarie, the three "inseparables," as the other girls called them, were returning from class under one umbrella, although they in fact had two more with them. Nevertheless, they found being squeezed under one umbrella very agreeable, even though they got awfully wet.

"Three little worms under one little umbrella," laughed Annemarie, making a mighty leap over a puddle. The other two girls, naturally, had to make the same jump.

"Do you remember, Annemie, when you didn't want to be with me under the same umbrella?" asked Vera half-seriously, half jokingly. She had finally mastered the German guttural rrr and didn't sound so foreign.

With a plaintive glance, Annemarie placed her wet hand on her mouth. She didn't want to be reminded of that dreadful time.

"Be careful!" A lady street cleaner had just missed the umbrella with her shovel, causing more laughing and hopping.

"Holy ding dong, now there are female street cleaners, and I recently saw a lady coach driver," said Annemarie happily.

"Even in the department stores there are lady elevator operators all over," said Margot.

"And in the streetcars and subways all I see are lady conductors—"

"If the war lasts any longer, there will be a policewoman rather than a policeman on the street corner," added Annemarie in high spirits.

"Really, it's not something to laugh about. The situation is very serious," said Margot deliberately. "A very nice female postman comes to our house. She has small children at home who are not being taken care of during the day while she is at work, all to get through this difficult time."

"Yes the time is difficult," said Annemarie with comic seriousness. She thought of the bread with marmalade that had replaced the buttered rolls at breakfast. "But I don't like the lady postman. She hasn't brought us a single letter from mommy. We've been waiting so long for another message."

"The lady postman can't do anything about that, Annemie," said Margot.

"In the end, it's the flying bombs falling on London ever more often that are preventing German letters from getting out, according to my brother Hans. Oh, if only I were a lady letter carrier's child, who at least had her mother mornings and evenings," said Annemarie.

Figure 10. "Three little worms under one little umbrella," laughed Annemarie, making a mighty leap over a puddle. (In German this phrase rhymes: Drei Würmchen unter einem Schirmchen.)

"What should I say first, Annemie!" Vera said softly.

Annemarie pressed her arm tenderly. "You're right, Vera, I'm a completely ungrateful rascal."

At noon, when Annemarie sat with her steaming soup, she heard in the courtyard below a child's thin voice, begging for a few pennies, accompanied by her mother's lute. As Nesthäkchen tossed down some coins, she thought, "If I could only be near my dear mommy, how gladly I would sing in courtyards during this miserable weather."

Grandmother pitied the young singing girl. "Call the child to come up, Annemie. We still have a bowl of soup left. The poor thing probably hasn't had anything warm to eat the entire day."

Annemarie happily carried out Grandmother's instructions. A good granddaughter is always glad to help.

"The mother has come too. The poor lady is blind. And the little worm is soaked to the skin," said Hanne.

"Heavens, we don't have enough soup for two. If only we had eaten less," said Grandmother regretfully.

"Grandma, I'll give up my soup, please let me," said Nesthäkchen sympathetically. She had just envied the beggar girl for having a mother. And the mother was blind.

Grandmother had no objection to Annemarie's sacrifice. It didn't hurt a child to give up something to help the poor.

Annemarie personally carried her almost full soup bowl into the kitchen and watched exultantly as the hungry singer ate. Fräulein had to bring Nesthäkchen back to the table.

Hans suggested, "We should eat less meat and vegetables, so the poor will have more."

"Bravo, Hans," said Grandmother. Even Klaus harbored the praiseworthy impulse to curb his appetite, which was not very difficult when cabbage confronted him.

Hanne could not accustom herself to the thrift that the war demanded of the household. She brought in a pancake. When Klaus saw it, he wanted to eat it himself. "I think that beggar girl is full now."

"Phooey, Klaus, said Nesthäkchen forcefully, "the poor thing has seen and smelled the pancake. It will be terrible if she can't have some."

"Yes, darling, but we won't have much if we have to cut another two portions from it," said Grandmother dubiously eyeing the pancake. "Hanne made enough for six servings. Of course, I will gladly give up mine—"

"I will give up mine," said Annemarie, although it wasn't easy. Because of her sweet tooth, she loved pancakes.

Hans agreed to give up his portion. But Klaus grumbled, "The crab will get too used to good food."

Nesthäkchen quickly carried pancake to her guest, before regret could set in. Seeing the girl's joy, she took pride in the sacrifice she had made.

What had happened?

When Nesthäkchen returned to the table, she found at her place a plate full of pancake. Nobody would say how it got there. Everyone whom Nesthäkchen suspected of giving up his or her portion was full of denial. Klaus turned out to be the benign donor, though he generally thought solely of his own stomach.

"You know, Grandma," said Nesthäkchen, "the beggar girl could eat here more often. The whole week she has had only coffee and dry bread for lunch. If all of us ate a little less, we'd still be full, and there would be enough left over for her. Every day Vera's aunt has a war child at table. The Thielens have an entire family twice a week.

Grandmother, who did her good deeds without fanfare, was prepared. "I must speak with the woman, so that we don't invite someone who is unworthy," she said.

What a miserable life that blind woman had. Quietly standing behind Grandmother, Nesthäkchen listened to the lady's story with tears in her eyes. The husband was dead. The woman had eked out a meager living caning chairs until the war began. Now there was no work. The high price of food sent mother and child to bed hungry. The few groschen that Trude earned singing in courtyards barely paid the rent.

Grandmother swung into action. She sent the soaked, shivering Trude with Fräulein and Annemarie to the nursery for dry clothes.

Since Reich wool week had begun, Annemarie had grown considerably. Trude, despite being thirteen, was small and thin.

Trude soon had boots on her feet to replace her old shoes, which had holes. She got a warm woolen dress from Annemarie. Klaus, who had a hood to protect him from the rain, gave her a loden cape that he had outgrown. Grandmother and Fräulein gave warm clothing to the mother.

As the grateful mother and child left to brave the cold November rain, courtyard to courtyard, Doctor's Nesthäkchen thought, "By what right do I have a better life than they do?"

Trude appeared at the Braun's table every day. At first Hanne, behaving like a manorial cook, carped that the "beggar-folk" would dirty her immaculate kitchen with their wet muddy feet. But as each day passed, she became more reconciled to the family's guest.

Trude was a darling girl and her own suffering had made her quite compassionate. Thankful for her lunch, she helped Hanne dry the dishes, ran errands, and did other small tasks. She took home food for her mother. Grandmother, who never did things by half, made sure that the impoverished blind lady received wool garments from her knitting society. Grandmother paid generously for every pair of stockings. Indeed, the society wanted to help the poor, even though it was not a charity. The blind woman herself joined the knitting society and was able to knit faster than most women with two good eyes. She began earning so much that Trude did not need to sing in courtyards.

Often, Annemarie invited the war child into her nursery. Trude was a well-brought-up, mannerly girl. Grandmother and Fräulein had nary a complaint about her. So the child of privilege and the child of poverty sat together during the long winter afternoons and knitted for the men in field gray. The war had fostered comradeship between rich and poor at the front and in the nursery as well.

Despite everything, a residuum of prejudice and vain pride was lodged in Nesthäkchen's heart.

This winter, Annemarie and her five girlfriends formed a small circle, and gathered for coffee every Saturday. They either knitted for the soldiers or sewed frocks with Fräulein's help for their Young Girls' Helpers Society. Those were lovely afternoons. One girl would tell engaging stories as the others worked diligently. Vera's pale cheeks reddened with eagerness, and joy returned to her eyes when she was among her high-spirited companions.

Today the circle was to meet at Annemarie's house. She had cleaned her room herself and personally set the table. Because Grandmother was expecting guests, the girls would drink their coffee in the nursery. Annemarie told Trude that she would be most grateful if Trude would bring a winter bouquet of fir and red berries, since Trude often ran errands for a flower shop. The bouquet would make a festive table centerpiece.

It was four o'clock. The girlfriends would soon arrive. Annemarie stood at her window looking excitedly at Margot's apartment. Margot was always first.

There was a soft knocking.

"Come in," said Annemarie, dashing for the door, thinking it was Margot.

The thin face of the war child was staring at her.

"If it's OK with you, Annemarie, can I stay here this afternoon? Mother doesn't need me," said Trude quietly.

Annemarie's face reddened. She didn't want to hurt Trude, but her request was out of the question.

Trude did not fail to notice Annemarie's hesitation. Then she saw the festively decked table with six settings.

"Oh, you're having guests, excuse me, I didn't know. Of course, I don't want to disturb you," said Trude, curtseying amicably and withdrawing.

Nesthäkchen felt odd. Had she done the wrong thing?

"Trude is a war child who was singing for pennies in our courtyard. I can't invite her to drink coffee with my girlfriends," she said to herself, trying to assuage her conscience.

But she didn't feel any better. Could Trude help it that her parents were poor? Wasn't she to be praised because she sang during rainstorms to help her blind mother earn a living? How politely she accepted her dismissal, without a trace of offense. Oh, it wouldn't have been so bad to ask the war child to stay for the party. Nesthäkchen's good side had taken the upper hand.

Annemarie felt strange indeed. She was happy, yet had spewed out vain pride. How could she attend her own party now? Every time she looked at Trude's winter bouquet, her happiness was transmuted into seriousness and reflection. What harm would it have done to have the war child here among the other girls? For the child herself it would have been a happy day in her life of poverty.

The Christmas frock for Mäxchen was finished. Everyone tried to decide what she should make next. Annemarie declared, "If Fräulein will be so good as to help us, I would like to sew a Sunday dress for our war child. Trude has the dress that I have outgrown, which she must wear weekdays and Sundays. What do you think?"

"Oh, Annemarie, we'll never be able to finish such a large dress," said Margot.

"What's so difficult? The seams are longer, that's all," said Ilse.

"Mommy sewed me a lovely dress, very simple, with sleeves cut from the same piece of cloth. It's easy with a pattern," added Marianne.

Marlene and Vera wanted to take part.

Annemarie's Fräulein was no spoiler. She declared herself ready to supervise the work and finish the parts that required the sewing machine.

"I'll contribute the fabric. Aunt Albertinchen gave me money yesterday for an opera ticket to see *Hänsel and Gretel*. I'm sure that if I ask her whether I can use the money to buy fabric for Trude's dress, she will let me," said Annemarie, feeling that the heavy burden weighing her down the entire afternoon had been lifted. She could now look at the war child's winter bouquet without remorse.

But a crucial question remained. What color should the dress be? The impractical girls were for pale blue. They finally acceded to Fräulein's suggestion that Trude would be better off with a red dress.

Next day the noon guest did not arrive. Hanne kept the lunch warm, but the war child never showed up. When Trude didn't come the following day, either, Grandmother said, "Something's not right. I'll send Hanne to her house with the lunch and ask what's wrong."

Annemarie's conscience bothered her. Was Trude not going to come again because she was angry? Nesthäkchen enlisted Fräulein to accompany her and find out.

The following afternoon, the two wandered through narrow, dirty lanes that the weak December light did not illuminate.

"Does Trude live here?" asked Annemarie, involuntarily turning up her nose as she entered a decrepit, uninviting abode.

The narrow courtyard was teaming with children. Annemarie had to make her way through them to reach the tenement across the way, where the war child lived.

"Pooh—the air here is awful," said Annemarie, holding her nose as she went up the old rickety stairs.

Fräulein knocked on a door at the top of four steps. A tiny boy with a mush-smeared face opened the door. Annemarie looked through steam emanating from laundry in the kitchen, and saw a woman standing at a washtub.

Fräulein asked about Trude's mother.

"Fritze, get the lady the information," said the woman as she labored over the laundry.

The mush-smeared Fritze lunged into a dark passageway. He opened a series of doors, screaming, "Frau Lehmann, you have visitors."

Nesthäkchen cringed fearfully behind Fräulein and became very anxious entering the dark, narrow, impoverished room. Yet the room was also neat and clean. At the window, where a pot of primroses bloomed, the blind woman sat knitting. Trude lay nearby on a bed made out of two wooden chairs.

When Trude saw Fräulein and Annemarie, her pale face looked happy.

"Please don't get up, Frau Lehmann," said Fräulein to the blind woman, who had risen politely from her chair. "We are stopping by for a moment to find out what happened to our noon guest. Why don't we see Trude any more?"

"Do you have a bad foot?" asked Annemarie fearfully when she saw the girl's tightly bandaged left leg.

"I fell when I left your house and broke my leg," said Trude.

"Oh, you poor child. Do you have much pain? Have you seen a doctor?" said Fräulein sympathetically.

"Yes, the doctor for the poor people was here. He advised bed rest. I am supposed to see him again."

Nesthäkchen, once so pert and talkative, did not say a word. If only she had not sent Trude away on that last afternoon. There had been an evening thaw, and had Trude left later she certainly would not have fallen.

"Wouldn't it be better if you were in a regular bed, Trude? You must be so uncomfortable on those chairs," said Fräulein.

"I have no bed," said Trude, blushing to the roots of her light blond hair.

"We must buy one, even though things are going so badly for us," said the blind woman. "Since her injury, Trude has been sleeping on straw. I wish, with her injured leg, she would use my bed, but she refuses."

Dear God—was Trude so impoverished that she didn't have a bed? There wasn't even a sofa in the room, just a few miserable pieces of furniture, and in the corner some straw on the ground. Annemarie was anguished. She was seeing real poverty for the first time. And she was responsible for Trude's plight, on account of her willfulness.

"I'll be back soon, Trude, very soon," said Nesthäkchen as she left.

Annemarie was as good as her word. In order to visit Trude, she overcame her aversion to the dark filthy tenement filled with the stink of poverty. She brought Trude an interesting book, a delicious apple, and a piece of cake, of which she had deprived herself. Doctor's Nesthäkchen had learned to think of others.

The day after Nesthäkchen's first visit, Grandmother sent an old sofa-bed from her own home to Trude's impoverished room. From now on, Trude was not forced to sleep on straw. Every evening Hanne brought the blind woman and her daughter food for the next day. She did this of her own accord, because "a person also has a heart in her body."

To illuminate the wartime darkness, the Brauns provided a Christmas tree with candles for Trude's room, along with a basket of food and useful items. On top was the pretty red dress that Annemarie and her friends had sewn for the war child.[4]

---

4. This description of Dickensian poverty is quite accurate. By 1900 Berlin had more slums than any other city in the world. The poor lived in unhealthy, inadequate, dilapidated tenements. Between 1800 and 1900 the population of Berlin had more than doubled. There were a million homes in the city, of which 400,000 had only one room, another 300,000 two rooms. Unheated rooms were not included in these statistics. It was not unusual for five people to live in a single room. The narrow courtyards and alleys contributed to the danger of devastating fires and the unhealthy conditions to frighteningly high infant mortality. (*Chronik Berlin*. Chronik Verlag, Munich 1997 pp 1903-1904.)

CHAPTER 18

▼

BUTTER POLONAISE

England's plan to starve out Germany by blocking food imports gradually made itself felt. Foodstuffs, especially fats, became scarce. But despite their disgraceful plot, the English were not able to use famine to drive the Germans to conclude a shameful peace. The German people held out, even after butter had completely disappeared from their bread. They would continue to hold out, even if the two meatless weekdays should turn into seven.

Like the men at the front, the women and children stood fast, ready to make any sacrifice, all possessed by the same goal: victory.

Thanks to the providence and intervention of the government, supplies had been husbanded so that Germany could hold out for years if necessary.[1] There

---

1. In fact, Germany had made no plans to husband supplies. The Germans had expected to crush the French with a single decisive blow, as they had in 1870. With the failure of their military plan (the Schlieffen plan) all stored food was quickly consumed during the first months of the war. Governmental officials immediately took charge of food distribution. But the British sea blockade and extremely poor harvests brought high prices and rationing. The situation reached crisis proportions in the winter of 1916/17, the so-called "turnip winter." The potato harvest was down by fifty percent, and many people were reduced to eating rutabagas. This unexpected catastrophe decimated the health of the German people, and a shortage of labor, fertilizer, and draft animals reduced the 1917 wheat harvest by half. By summer 1917 Germans were consuming 1,000 calories daily, on average, rather than the 2,280 which public health authorities declared was the minimum necessary. Hunger was most prevalent in the big cities. As war profiteers became rich, 750,000 Germans died of starvation and malnutrition between 1914 and 1918.

were bread and grain ration cards, egg, butter, sugar, and meat ration cards, milk ration cards, even soap ration cards. Because of the hassle, people had to think hard about every purchase, which sometimes wasn't easy.[2]

Grandmother had formerly enjoyed doing some of the household chores. But the ration cards were too much for her. She couldn't brave crowds or long lines.

Grandma tried standing on line once but never again. After an extended wait, she pulled the sugar card instead of the milk card out of her bag. When she tried to rectify her error, she only managed to produce meat cards and potato cards. She had to haul out her glasses, a dubious proposition for an older person. The teeming mass of people behind her became annoyed. The saleslady became impatient and impolite. No, Grandmother would not go shopping again.

Fräulein usually accepted this task, as Hanne was busy taking care of the house. But during Dr. Braun's consulting hours, it was difficult for Fräulein to leave. Patients were always coming who didn't know that Dr. Braun was at the front, and Fräulein had to send these people to another doctor. She was better at doing this than anyone else.

So Nesthäkchen often had the honorable job of procuring groceries for the Braun household. She did not mind standing in front of a store for hours. It was a pity that after patient waiting she did not return home with the desired item. And simply because the forgetful girl had left the necessary card on the nursery table.

The children, who did not appreciate the seriousness of the times, enjoyed making fun of the so called "butter polonaise." People would stand, four abreast, in lines a block long, hour after hour to buy a half-pound of butter. But sometimes after a long wait in the winter cold, the prospective purchaser would find that the butter was sold out.

Despite these difficulties and sacrifices, the German people's will to hold out had not weakened.

---

2. Else Ury does not mention the flourishing black market, which created considerable anger, envy, and bitterness. In late 1915 wealthy people were feasting in splendor in Berlin's Hotel Esplanade, with no difficulty about ration cards. On meatless days, the elegant Hotel Adlon served chicken, duck, and other fowl not considerd meat. In spring 1916 an American traveler had "a most royal dinner" in the mansion of the prominent banker Max Warburg, "roast beef...and many courses," nectarines from Warburg's hothouse in the country, and "big glorious strawberries with plenty of sugar." In the army, officers had first call on food, wines, and liquors filched from occupied territories. (Asprey, Robert. The German High Command at War. William Morrow. New York 1991, p 259)

Grandmother would not permit Nesthäkchen to stand in long lines during rainstorms. The girl might get a cold. Klaus could better withstand inclement weather, as he was a strong boy. But Klaus didn't have much patience. He made himself unpopular by jostling other people standing near him. And instead of walking to the end of the line, he would try to cut in front, with unhappy results. The policeman who kept the butter polonaise orderly pulled Klaus out of line by his ear and wouldn't let him back in. After this contretemps Klaus no longer went to buy butter. He preferred to eat marmalade bread with cheese or sausage.

Certainly the young were able to manage. But Grandmother could not do without her bread and butter. Nesthäkchen took care of this need faithfully. After meals, when Grandmother had her nap, Nesthäkchen put on warm shoe covers, a fur hat and muff. Dressed like a polar explorer, she went to buy butter. She often agreed to meet Margot and Vera. In the society of her friends, the waiting was not so onerous.

"OK, at 3:30 we'll meet at Savignyplatz for the butter polonaise," Annemarie shouted to her friends as she left school.

It was snowing heavily. The snowflakes were falling thick and fast. It was hard for anyone to keep her eyes open. People on the streets looked like snowmen.

Nevertheless, a long line was snaking down the street when Nesthäkchen arrived at the butter store on the corner. She was covered with white powdery snow, but buying the butter came first. People had been standing in line since noon. Many were sitting on little chairs they had brought along. Here and there a diligent lady knitted a field gray stocking for a far-off husband or son, doing the best she could with her clammy fingers.

Nesthäkchen could not find Vera. Had she stayed home because of the bad weather? Margot had already excused herself for this reason. Fräulein too did not want to allow Annemarie to leave the house. But she had finally conceded that Nesthäkchen was not made of sugar; a little snow would not soften her. In the Baltic, she had become inured to the worst kinds of weather. And since Grandmother had had no butter for breakfast, Annemarie wanted to surprise her at dinner.

Vera never arrived. As Annemarie waited, the line grew longer minute by minute. It had never been so long. Nesthäkchen might have to wait two to three hours.

This thought did not frighten Annemarie. She was quite comfortable with the butter polonaise. The people were all companions in suffering and stood allied with one another. And since there was nothing else to do, people entertained themselves by talking about the war and the economy. The women exchanged recipes that did not require fats, or they read post cards from the front that their relatives had written. In all, Annemarie usually found the butter polonaise quite diverting.

But today the butter polonaise became quite disagreeable. The fine snow, which Nesthäkchen had enjoyed at first, began to penetrate her clothes and chill her. Despite her overshoes, and despite the fact that she jumped from one foot to another in the narrow confines, her feet were freezing.

"Oh, it's no pleasure to be in a trench at the front in weather like this. I'd rather have a snowflake hit my nose than a bullet," said the lady greengrocer from around the corner, who had planted her formidable bulk right next to Annemarie.

Everyone laughed and didn't feel inconvenienced by the weather any longer. At least for a while.

Imperceptibly, the line moved forward. Annemarie used this opportunity to memorize the poem that she had been assigned to learn in German class that morning, Schiller's *Bell*,[3] and declaimed the poet's words with spirit:

> *When the copper is molten,*
> *Add the tin quickly*

"No, Frau Schulzen, when it's cooking, add a little egg substitute and it will look like you've put in at least three egg yolks," said a woman nearby.

> *Madness is short, rue is long.*

"The rows have never been so long," said someone else. Annemarie became confused whether the word she should memorize was *rue* or *row*.

> *A man must go out*
> *In a hostile world—*

"Yes, he has to get out, he hasn't been standing in line, he has to start from the end—"

The conversations around her were becoming so interesting that Annemarie interrupted her studies.

---

3. Friedrich von Schiller (1759-1805) *Das Lied von der Glocke* (The Song of the Bell)

"Look, it's starting to rain—"
Annemarie began reciting her Schiller again enthusiastically,

The blessing gushes out of the cloud,
The rain streams down—

"My feet have turned to ice in front of this butter store. Three cheers for mealtimes. Butter is everything," came from Annemarie's left.

The place is burnt to cinders,

murmured Nesthäkchen,

lovely peace, sweet harmony,
waft amicably over this city!

"Do you think we'll have war with America?"
No, it was not possible to memorize Schiller amidst all the commotion. Annemarie gave up.
"Männe, it's good you've come to relieve me. Now I'm going to warm up the inner me with a drop of hot coffee," said the fat lady green grocer, who left the line as her red-haired son took her place.
Oh, if Annemarie had only thought of getting Klaus to relieve her. How gladly she would have warmed up, too. Indeed, it was getting colder. The fat lady with her broad back had shielded Annemarie from the wind, but Männe was thin and an inadequate windshield.
Nesthäkchen reached the store entrance. She was first in line and, filled with expectation, she no longer felt the cold. The policeman counted off the rows. Annemarie was almost there.
Hurrah! She got a half-pound of butter. She never would have thought that such a thing could give her so much pleasure. During war you learn to treasure everything.
Her half-pound of butter pressed against her heart, Annemarie hurried out of the store, as people still in line looked on enviously. Now to have coffee at home in a cozy room.
Nesthäkchen heard a tremulous voice. "Oh, God, I can't take it anymore. I think I'm going to faint." It was an old man who could hardly stand up.

"Go home. Old people shouldn't wait for hours in this weather," people shouted at him.

"I would give up butter myself, but my grandchild is very sick. The doctor says he has to eat well, if we want to keep him alive."

Curious, Annemarie had stopped to listen to the tale of woe.

She wavered. The man was a grandfather, who was standing on line for his grandchild in a snowstorm for hours on end. What if Grandma had to freeze like this?

"Here, please," she said pleasantly to the man, "take my butter and go home. I'm young. I can stand out in the cold for another half hour."

"Thank you. A thousand thanks. You are a noble child. God will reward you for your deed," said the man, paying Annemarie for her butter. As the people nearby murmured their approval, Annemarie took the old man's place in line.

Strangely, she felt the cold, snow, and rain less. The thought of having done a good deed warmed her from within.

A small hooded figure in the line pushed forward, her loden cape pulled up to her nose.

"Annemarie!" came a voice from beneath the hood as the girl approached. "Annemarie, you must go home. Your Grandmother is looking for you. I will take your place in line."

"No, Trude, you have a sick leg. You can't stand very long. But many thanks," said Annemarie.

"Oh, my leg is much better. I don't notice it at all now. Go home."

"But I'm dressed much more warmly than you. You'll freeze," said Annemarie hesitantly.

Trude laughed.

"I've had to freeze before. And the poor children in my building, who have to get into the meat line in the middle of the night, can stand more cold than this."

Annemarie pressed Trude to take her overshoes and muff before dashing home sneezing, as fast as her feet could carry her.

"Achoo! Achoo!" Annemarie had to laugh. The reward for her good deed would surely be a formidable head cold. Yet it really wasn't necessary for almighty God to repay her. Her knowledge that she had helped the old man was adequate compensation.

Fräulein gave Nesthäkchen warm stockings and shoes. Hanne brought her steaming cocoa. Then Grandmother handed the dear, naughty child, who had stood so long in a snowstorm, a letter on very thin paper.

"From mommy, my mommy, finally," said Annemarie, kissing the neat handwriting, which she hadn't seen for months.

Mother was hopeful that she would receive permission to return home. When Annemarie had finished reading, there was stunned silence. The greatest joy is expressed silently, not loudly. Overwhelmed with ecstasy, Annemarie pressed her head to Grandmother's breast.

Didn't almighty God reward each good deed?

CHAPTER 19

▼

GERMAN SUMMER TIME

Mäxchen, the Young Girls' Helpers child, ran around the courtyard and yelled "Tatta" when Annemarie appeared at the window. This word meant *aunt* in Mäxchen's language. The Berlin refugee office had no word about his parents, nor had Hans been able to discover anything. They had probably been victims of the Cossacks.

At Easter Hans had left the family home. He passed his final examinations and despite Grandmother's reservations had joined the navy and was in training at Wilhelmshaven.

Klaus had advised his brother to join the air force. Since early childhood, Klaus had shown a partiality to flying. In fact, he had often rudely "flown" out of rooms himself.

Nesthäkchen was sorrowful when she said goodbye to her dear Hänschen. As proud as she was that Hans would be serving the fatherland, she wouldn't have him nearby when she wanted him. She redoubled her efforts to knit her brother warm garments to shield him from North Sea storms.

Annemarie had more to do in school. At Easter she entered the fourth class, where many demands were made on the students.

During the two war years, the thirteen-year-old Annemarie had become a gorgeous girl. The serious times had washed away the few cinders of conceit and vanity that clung to the pampered child. They had made her more selfless and helpful. Despite her gaiety and devilishness, she was an intelligent young lady.

Externally Annemarie had also developed well. She was taller than Grandma, and her tousled blond braids hung down to her back.

In spite of the food shortage, Annemarie had bloomed like a May rose. Her long sojourn in the Baltic had not been in vain.

At home, everyone could see the good effect the war years had had on Doctor's Nesthäkchen. Her loving attention to Grandmother was touching. Nesthäkchen was now old enough to see what a sacrifice Grandmother had made. She had exchanged the quiet comfort of her own home for the tense, noisy environs of her grandchildren.

It was April 30, 1916, a strange day. Actually, it was the night of May 1st. People had to move the clock hands.

Time had set its own pace since the creation. Now men dared to bring it in step with them. Throughout Germany, on the night of May 1st all clocks were to be set forward one hour. During the summer months the day would begin one hour sooner, saving the energy needed for an hour of artificial light, as well as copper wire, coal, and petroleum. The time change was part of a new war economy.

Grandma was disoriented. In the past months, she had had to learn to do things in ways to which she was not accustomed. But she was simply not able to get into her old head that the war could reset the clock.

"I'm old fashioned. I'll continue to live the way I have for almost seventy years," she said.

"Me, oh, gracious lady, I can't get accustomed to the disruption," said Hanne. "If it's six, it's not seven. No, I'm not yet completely crazy."

Annemarie left school arm in arm with Margot and Vera. To the young, big changes are fun.

"I hope I don't oversleep tomorrow. I want to arrive at school on time at seven," said Margot.

"You mean at eight," laughed Annemarie.

"OK, but tomorrow we have the new time." The girls giggled. The whole thing could confuse anyone.

"I stayed in bed an hour earlier today," said Vera.

"I wouldn't in my dreams have thought this would happen. I want to go to the city hall with Klaus at eleven PM. Klaus told me that we would see it get to be one hour later. That will be fantastic."

"Oh, will your Grandmother allow you out so late?" asked Margot.

"I can take care of myself, and I want to. So goodbye until we see each other tomorrow on German summer time. Hurrah! We'll all be an hour older." The three friends parted gaily.

After lunch, Klaus waved at his sister with a knowing look.

"So, Annemarie, are you coming with me tonight to see the city hall clock moved ahead?"

"Oh, Kläuschen, Grandmother would never, never permit it—"

"Of course, if you're stupid enough to ask," said Klaus, the villain, looking at his sister with contempt.

"Fräulein will surely notice if I go," said Annemarie, burning with desire to accompany Klaus.

"Nonsense with sauce, Fräulein snores like a sawmill. If you don't want to come, OK. I'll go by myself. But let me say something to you: You won't see anything like this in your entire life. The time change is an earth-shaking event. It is the duty of every educated person to be a witness." Klaus was so convincing. Nesthäkchen decided she must not waver.

"I'll see. If Fräulein is asleep, maybe I'll come along," said Annemarie.

The entire afternoon Nesthäkchen was in turmoil. She was hardly able to gather her thoughts to do her homework.

Should she or shouldn't she?

That night the shadow of German summer time fell over the rebellious Braun household.

Fräulein set the dinner table.

"Is it already so late, Fräulein?" asked Grandmother.

"Five minutes to eight. Hanne is about to bring in the milk noodles."

The female family members took their places at table. Klaus never arrived on time. Grandmother rang for the meal, although she wasn't very hungry.

The cook appeared with a puzzled face and no milk noodles. "Yes, what does this mean? Today is not yet tomorrow. I'm not taking part in this crazy business. I've just started making the noodles," grumbled the kitchen fairy.

Hanne had been working for the family many years, and her grumbling did not bother them. Even if she was sometimes too blunt, she meant well.

"Look at the time, Hanne. It's almost eight," said Grandma, pointing to the grandfather clock in the corner.

"My kitchen clock says seven," growled Hanne.

"Then go by the time out here," said Fräulein "The clocks in the living room and the doctor's consulting room are striking eight."

"If you want my opinion, we can ignore this new fangled summer time. No one should eat dinner for another hour," said Hanne, angrily disappearing.

"Sometimes Hanne can't deal with the war. If I tell her there's too much fat in the food, she takes it as a personal affront. Every war economy measure goes against her nature," sighed Grandmother.

"She doesn't mean any harm," said Nesthäkchen in defense of her old friend.

Nesthäkchen was right. Hanne's outburst was paining her. A half hour later the noodles were on the table.

"I should have served them sooner," said Hanne apologetically.

Grandmother's appetite was returning. One should enjoy dinner during wartime. Only Klaus, who was with a friend, was missing.

"The boy should be here. It is 8:30," said Fräulein shaking her head.

"Yes, he could at least think about being punctual for meals," said Grandmother.

Annemarie didn't say anything, although she was concerned. Had Klaus already gone to the city hall to get a good place to witness the spectacle?

No, there he was at the door, whistling as though he had done nothing wrong. The clocks in the house struck nine.

"Hello, have you already eaten?" he asked puzzled.

"Now listen to me, my boy. You can't demand that we alter our mealtimes. I must ask you to be punctual," said Grandmother forcefully.

"I have never been so punctual as today," said Klaus.

"Yes?" said all three females, looking reproachfully at the clock.

"Thunder and lightning! I forgot all about it," said Klaus as he laughed loudly. "I set our clocks ahead today, so that we could accustom ourselves to summer time gradually."

The others joined in his youthful laughter, even Hanne, who had to warm the noodles.

But when Klaus wanted to set her alarm clock ahead by an hour, Hanne put her foot down.

"Nobody touches my alarm clock. The whole world may be crazy, but I'm getting up at the same time as always."

"But Hanne, then we'll have to go to school without coffee," yammered Nesthäkchen.

"It serves you right for going by a botched up clock. I'll be up at seven, like always."

Despite Hanne, Fräulein promised to awaken the children promptly at seven. Everyone would go to bed an hour earlier so they could get up an hour earlier. After she had gotten Annemarie off to school, Fräulein could sleep until ten.

Annemarie suffered from a frightfully bad conscience when she gave grandmother her goodnight kiss.

"When the clock strikes eleven, get up quietly. It's really ten and we'll have enough time. I know where they keep the spare house key," Klaus whispered to Nesthäkchen.

Annemarie lay in bed and prayed, "Dear God, you haven't let mommy leave that old England. Do it now, please, please, in the new summer time." But she felt guilty. Good deeds were rewarded, bad ones were punished. Would God prevent mommy from coming home because Annemarie was sneaking out with Klaus? Maybe she shouldn't do it. But Klaus would think she was uneducated. "Dear God, let me be asleep when the clock strikes eleven," she pleaded.

And truly, it wasn't long before her long golden lashes closed over her blue eyes. Nesthäkchen slept soundly. She didn't hear the striking of the clock, or the furtive clatter of young feet at the nursery door.

"Annemarie, are you awake?" whispered Klaus.

No answer.

Klaus opened the door. He had promised to take his sister along. Also, it would be nice to have some company in the middle of the night.

"Annemarie, wake up," he said, tiptoeing to her bed to shake her arm gently.

Bang! He tripped over a chair in the darkness, which he threw aside with a loud oath.

Alarmed, Fräulein and Annemarie jumped up in unison.

"What's wrong?" said Fräulein as she switched on the light. In front of her stood Klaus in hat and coat with a stupid expression on his face.

"I—I," he stuttered, for the moment with no excuse.

Annemarie laughed. She couldn't help herself.

"Oh, Klaus, we have to confess," said Annemarie with relief. "You shouldn't become angry, Fräulein, you must promise me." Fräulein promised and Nesthäkchen confessed.

The "world-shaking event," the resetting of the city hall clock by one hour, occurred without the presence of the Braun offspring.

Next morning, though, they consecrated the new summer time by resetting the clocks that had not been reset the day before. Luckily, Klaus and Annemarie weren't the only children who were late for school. Indeed, half of the pupils were still not accustomed to summer time.

In the sky above, the May sun shone and laughed at the stupid people, who wanted to bungle her schedule. She and Doctor's Hanne knew better than anyone what hour the clock was actually striking.

Hanne got used to the new time more easily than anyone would have thought. She couldn't let "her" children leave for school without coffee. If at 7:30 in the evening they wanted to make a quick trip to the store, they could.

Although the rebellious Hanne had been forced to accept summer time, there were consolations. "It isn't so bad to see a fine May evening in the daytime."

People didn't think about the time change for very long, even Grandmother.

At home and at the front the new summer time reigned, and Germany's enemies soon adopted it as well.

The joyous month of May passed, and in June there was another ocean of flags fluttering in German cities, this time for the navy, the "blue-jackets." At Skagerrak, Germany's young fleet achieved a stunning victory over England's world-dominant sea power.[1]

"As soon as our Hänschen joined the navy, they had a big victory," rejoiced Doctor's Nesthäkchen.

She sat on her balcony under waving flags and wrote to her brother. The June sun shone, illuminating the victory banners and shimmering in Annemarie's golden blond hair. Nesthäkchen was filled with joy, and the sun knew why. She laughed into her palm and sent her rays through the window of a rattling train carriage arriving in Berlin. Inside, a slim blond lady, after a long absence, greeted the towers of her hometown with misty eyes.

Annemarie wrote and wrote, so extravagantly did the sunlight fall on her writing paper. Did the dumb Nesthäkchen suspect nothing?

---

1. The battle took place on 31 May 1916 off the Danish peninsula known as Jutland. The area of water in which the battle was fought is called the Skaggerak, which is the battle's German name. Many experts call this battle both the greatest and most controversial naval battle in history. The main controversy concerns who should be called the victor, the German High Seas Fleet, or the British Royal Navy's Grand Fleet. Many people say that the Germans won because, though outnumbered, they sank more ships and did more damage than the much larger British Grand Fleet. Others point out that the battle did nothing to impede the British blockade of Germany, a British "strategic victory". Though some historians say that the British won, it was the Germans who actually were victorious because of superior ship design, more reliable fire control, and safer gun charges.

A car clattered along the quiet street and stopped in front of the Braun's house. Annemarie raised her head and looked out with curiosity. An electric jolt passed through her young body.

"Mommy—my only mommy!" A shriek of joy rang out in the tranquil street like nothing anyone had ever heard.

In a few seconds, Nesthäkchen had dashed down the stairs and embraced her mother ardently.

"My Lotte, my Nesthäkchen, my dear little one, I have been deprived of you for so long." Mother and child could not let go of one another.

What did it mean to the two, who had been separated almost three years, that here and there curious faces appeared at windows, or that the taxi driver had to wait for his fare?

Scampering youthful feet, accompanied by the joyful whining of Puck, stormed down to the street. Mother released Nesthäkchen to embrace and kiss her curly brown-haired son.

Cars slowed down as their drivers stopped to stare. But the scene of passionate reunion made them happy.

With one child on each arm, Mrs. Braun entered her home. Grandmother stood at the bottom of the stairs, unable to wait until her daughter reached the top.

"Mommy, I thank you for giving me peace of mind, when I was so far from my country and my children," said Mrs. Braun as she embraced her mother.

Amidst the outpouring of joy, Nesthäkchen cried out in pain. In mommy's blond hair she saw a few silver threads illuminated by the sun in the stairway window. The difficult times in the enemy's country were the culprit. With her love, Nesthäkchen would wash away the evil memories.

Fräulein appeared with happy eyes as she grasped the banister.

At the top of the stairs Hanne smiled. "God be thanked that our gracious lady is with us again. Now maybe we'll get to the end of this awful war," she said.

"Whatever I can do to help, Hanne, that I will do," joked Mrs. Braun. The pain her long absence had caused in her home dissipated rapidly.

Outside, victory banners waved. Inside, in the comfortable living room, people sat happily reunited. The dear sun glowed along with Annemarie's eyes.

Mommy spoke, while she regarded her blooming Nesthäkchen, no longer her smallest, indeed as tall as she was herself. How could she thank God enough for permitting her to return home and for protecting her country and her family?

As the bells of Pentecost rang throughout the land, Father came home on leave. Everyone listened to the sonorous bells and felt what Mother said, "May the bells of peace soon ring throughout rejoicing Germany, God willing!"

*   *   *   *

With this wish I take my leave from you, my dear young readers. No doubt many of you, like Nesthäkchen, have made sacrifices, large and small, for the World War. But I am convinced that you have done so joyfully for our fatherland. When the heavy battle around us is at an end and we arrive at a victorious peace, I will tell you more about Doctor's Nesthäkchen. Until then, farewell!

EPILOGUE

▼

Why did Else Ury decide at this point, June 1916, not to write more about Nesthäkchen until peace was declared? Although no one can say for certain, the likely reason is that that the war had become pure slaughter, a Brobdingnagian meat grinder, an unmitigated disaster, and Else Ury could no longer bear to deal with it. The Battle of Verdun, which began in February 1916, was to claim the lives of 300,000 French and German soldiers. Before Verdun, Germany could have negotiated an armistice on highly favorable terms. Afterward this opportunity no longer existed. When peace did finally arrive after 1,500 days of fighting, millions of young men had died like butchered cattle, while millions more were wounded or hideously maimed. In Germany, famine and starvation had supplanted the butter polonaise.

"The hour has struck for the weighty settlement of our accounts," said Georges Clemenceau, the French Premier, to German Foreign Minister Count Ulrich von Brockdorff-Rantzau. The year was 1919. The First World War had ended with an armistice seven months before. The scene was the Hall of Mirrors in France's Versailles Palace, where Louis XIV, the Sun King, had once reigned.

The victorious Allies declared to the representatives of a defeated Germany that there were to be no negotiations. The Germans were simply to receive the terms that the Allies had agreed on.

The reception the vengeful French gave to Brockdorff-Rantzau, a thin, pale professional diplomat with a monocle, must have alerted him to expect the worst. They forced his special train, filled with 180 diplomats and experts preparing to argue the German case, to skulk along at ten miles an hour. The Germans were thus compelled to see the devastation their armies had inflicted on the countryside of northern France. In Versailles, the French housed the German delegation in an isolated hotel surrounded by barbed wire, and made them carry their own bags upstairs.

The French terms were harsh. Clemenceau demanded total payment for all of France's war damages, its five million dead and wounded, its 4,000 ruined towns and 20,000 destroyed businesses. He declared that the Germans must pay up to a hundred years if necessary, with interest. British experts calculated that the Germans owed a total of 800 billion marks, which was more than all the German national wealth.

The Allies summarily rejected a German counter-offer of 100 billion marks, without interest. Instead, they demanded an immediate initial payment of $5 billion in gold, along with considerable quantities of coal, chemicals, and shipping, to be delivered by May 1921. The final amount to be paid was left to future negotiations. Winston Churchill called the reparations "a sad story of complicated idiocy." They led to an unending dispute between Germany and the Allies, and were a partial cause for the ruinous German hyperinflation of 1923 that wiped out the savings of the middle class.

Else Ury, by passionately supporting the disastrous war, had in effect written her own death warrant. The lost war and the Versailles Treaty made possible the rise of Adolf Hitler. Had there been no war, Hitler probably would have spent his life as an obscure Munich painter of architectural scenes.

"Everyone wants to know if Nesthäkchen is a real person and where she lives," Else Ury wrote. "Yes, my Nesthäkchen lives. Where we work and strive, where our German fatherland and German earth benefit us, in the city and in the country, where we disperse luck and joy in our own dwellings—My Nesthäkchen is at home there."

But Else Ury herself was not at home there. The hatred of many Germans for their Jewish fellow citizens was simply too intense. Like the two million German men who sacrificed their lives in the war, Else Ury paid the ultimate price for her ardent love of Germany.

About the Illustrator

Robert Sedlacek, the most well known illustrator of the Nesthäkchen books, was Viennese. He was not only a professor, but also a highly successful commercial artist. His illustrations for Persil Washing Powder and Kölnisches Wasser cologne were on billboards throughout Germany. Sedlacek's Nesthäkchen illustrations have a subtle erotic quality. Women are gracious, flawless, slender, and flirtatious. They have an elegant fashion-consciousness, and Sedlacek emphasizes their femininity by often dressing them very sparsely. Their clothes have frequently slipped upward to reveal stimulating areas of skin, or their skin may show through their sheer garments. While Else Ury must have liked Sedlacek's work, with its hint of Weimar decadence, it was probably a bit too risqué for any German children's publisher after World War II. Rudolf Hengstenberg's 1950's illustrations in the present-day Nesthäkchen editions are boringly conventional by comparison, without a trace of Sedlacek's raciness.

References

BOOKS AND ARTICLES

- Anonymous. Else Urys Koffer nach Grenz-Querelen wieder in Museum Auschwitz. Deutsche Presse-Agentur (DPA)–Europadienst. August 29, 2002.

- Asprey, Robert. The German High Command at War. William Morrow. New York 1991, p 259.

- Bedürftig Friedemann. Nesthäkchens Koffer: Das Ende der Mädchenbuchautorin Else Ury im Vernichtungslager Auschwitz. Süddeutsche Zeitung. October 21, 1995

- Brentzel, Marianne. Nesthäkchen kommt ins KZ. Eine Annäherung an Else Ury 1877-1943. Fischer Taschenbuch Verlag. Frankfurt am Main 1992.

- Chronik Berlin. Chronik Verlag, Munich 1997 pp 1903-1904.

- Friedrich, Otto. Before the Deluge. Harper & Row. New York 1972.

- Keller, Heidi. Mutter aller Nesthäkchen. Else Ury wäre am 1. November 125 Jahre alt geworden. Aufbau. New York. Nov 14, 2002.

- Lehrer, Steven. Hitler Sites. McFarland. Jefferson, North Carolina 2002.

- Lehrer, Steven. Wannsee House and the Holocaust. McFarland. Jefferson, North Carolina 2000.

- Marshall, SLA. The American Heritage History of World War I. American Heritage Publishing. New York, 1964.

• Pech, Klaus-Ulrich: Ein Nesthaken als Klassiker. Else Urys *Nesthäkchen*-Reihe. In: Klassiker der Kinder-und Jugendliteratur. Edited by Bettina Hurrelmann. Fischer Verlag. Frankfurt/M. 1995, pp 339–357.

• Röhl, John C.G. Wilhelm II: der Aufbau des Persönlichen Monarchie. CH Beck. Munich 2001.

• Tagliaube, John. For France and Germany, still no love lost. New York Times. March 14, 2003 A3.

• Tuchman, Barbara. The Guns of August. Macmillan. New York 1962.

• Winter, Jay and Blaine Baggett. The Great War. Penguin Books. New York 1996.

• Zentner, Christian and Friedemann Bedürftig, eds. The Encyclopedia of the Third Reich. English translation edited by Amy Hackett. Macmillan, New York 1991.

WEBSITES

• Deutsches Historisches Museum. Der Erste Weltkrieg. Lebendiges Museum Online. www.dhm.de/lemo/html/wk1

• Duffy, Michael. First World War.com www.firstworldwar.com

978-0-595-39729-7
0-595-39729-8